A Great Big Fuss

an anthology of strange stories

from fOOfARAW PRESS

2025

Table of Contents

Introduction

Well this one has been quite the journey—as you might be able to tell from the 2025 on the cover, despite being published in 2026. Things are vastly different, both professionally and personally for us here at fOOfARAW HQ.

When we opened the call for this anthology, we had only been publishing fiction on the site for a few months and I was gainfully employed. By the time the call closed, we had almost all of 2025's stories for the site planned out, and a wealth of submissions to this anthology, but I was unemployed. So while there was a lot I wanted to do, money and motivation were at an all-time low.

It's safe to say things have vastly improved since then. fOOfARAW has continued to grow, and I like to think we've carved out a pretty nice place for ourselves in the litmag world and even built a bit of a reputation amongst both readers and writers.

While it obviously goes without being said, you would not be holding this book in your hand if not for all of the incredibly kind and patient writers who are featured in this anthology. I'm overjoyed that they've all continued to put their trust in me despite how long it's taken to get to this point, and incredibly proud of what we've been able to put together collectively and to have my name alongside all of these wonderful human beings.

With all that being said, we have a truly wonderful collection of fun, quirky, strange, weird, and fussy stories to share with you and I hope you enjoy every second of it.

Until next time,

—*Kevin Kortum*

Much Ado About Foofaraw
by Nicholas De Marino

foofaraw 🔊

[**foo**-*fuh*-raw] ⊙ Phonetic (Standard) ○ **IPA**

noun

1.   a great fuss about about something very insignificant...

No. You can't start like that. Not unless you're giving a commencement speech. Then definitions are totally fair game. Hackneyed? Sure, but preferable to allusion or allegory. Like when our high school valedictorian, Barbie (yes, really), yapped on and on about Gandhi and how we ought to live our lives. But she left out that thing about him sleeping in the same bed as his naked teenage grandnieces after his wife died. You know, so he could be a better person by not getting aroused. (How many flaccid nights in a row? Were these young ladies eligible for inner peace, too? Who was the big spoon? Don't ask me; I can't even pronounce *brahmacharya*.) To be fair, self-righteous celibacy would've been a tough sell to horny, soon-to-be-drunk teens.

Anyway, armchair etymology and memetics offer better insight into meaning. Particularly when it comes to "foofaraw."

This gem of a word was first recorded in America on the western frontier, probably in the early to mid-19th century, depending whom you ask. We're talking the Mexican-American War. We're talking the displacement and massacre of indigenous peoples. (If you enjoy Manifest Destiny and implied nip slips, check out the painting

"American Spirit" by John Gast. The cigarettes of a similar name and fakelore imagery came later.) We're talking simmering Civil War tensions. We're talking California gold rush. (John Berkey—the artist who made the poster for Star Wars—did a painting of this for a commemorative postage stamp. The design team doctored the image to include a black guy.) Plus Mormons and wagon trails. ("You have died of dysentery." R.I.P. Mouthface.) And don't forget those Chinese railroad workers.

It's a storied area that makes much of its own history. Especially in rural Wyoming. When I was a newspaper reporter there, I saw my share of jackalopes, ghost towns, and "hog ranch" whorehouse ruins. There was frontier justice and the boots to match. (Actual, human-skin boots, worn by a governor on inauguration day. "They used to have nipples," said a lady at the museum.) There was a historical missing person case sometimes attributed to a likely serial killer. And there was a more recent missing person who I had a strong hunch got disappeared by a certain authority figure in town. Homie handled a spouse-beater like ranchers handle rogue wolves: shoot, shovel, and shut up.

Now where was I?

"Foofaraw" might be from Spanish: fanfarrón, meaning braggart or boaster. (That, in turn, might go back to Arabic: farfār, for talkative.) There were plenty of Spanish-speaking ranch hands busting balls and bulls in the area. They're the OG cowboys, after all. Old West lingo takes a saddlebagful of cues from half-heard Spanish, especially on the rancho. (Detour back to French, then maybe Frankish, then a Proto-Germanic word for curve or ring.) That's how we got things like "buckaroo," "lasso," "lariat," "chaps," and "rodeo," as well as a "stampede" of eggcorns according to pedantic etymology sites, adverb-free listicles, and source-robbing A.I. (I'm just plain old source-robbing I.)

Meanwhile, back at the ranch, "foofaraw" might've arrived via French, which has *fanfaron* as well as a dialect form, *fanfarou*, meaning pretty much the same thing as the related Spanish.

It's hard to be sure about any of this, really. That's too bad. I wanted to make this explanation a definitive guide. (Alternate spellings include foofarah, foofooraw, and fooforaw.) But somehow this whole thing has turned into a giant load of foofaraw.

Nicholas De Marino needs a hug. Poetry in Dreams & Nightmares and Horrific Scribblings. Fiction in BULL and Hell Itself. Monthly columns (fnord) in foofaraw and The Independent Variable. ¡Viva SFPA y Codex! No awards but some nominations.

More at nicholasdemarino.blogspot.com.

Mind the Gap
by Matthew R. Davis

Braden saw the warning that would change everything at the train station—of all places—as his family hobbled forward to board their carriage. Three words, stern and simple and strange, stenciled in white paint at the edge of the platform.

MIND THE GAP

He asked his mother what it meant and she pointed out what should have been obvious even to a ten-year-old: the message was alerting passengers to the slight distance between the steel lip of the train's entrance and the cement edge of the platform. Braden shuddered to think what might happen should this warning go unheeded, his young mind conjuring up all sorts of gooshy nastiness as he imagined the gap sucking people down into its narrow jaws. He made sure to take an extra-large step when boarding the train, heaving a mammoth sigh of relief when he didn't slip and fall into the crack. He'd done it. He'd *minded the gap*.

But now that he'd been exposed to them, those three words burrowed into his brain like an infectious pop song. They continued to pound inside his head in counterpoint to the clatter of the train's wheels on the tracks, echoing the rhythm of Queen's "We Will Rock You": *mind the gap, mind the gap, mind the gap*. And it didn't escape him that those three syllables required a silence on the fourth beat to complete the groove—a gap, you could say. That silence loomed in his skull whenever he let the beat fall quiet, a gap that grew ever wider and deeper with every second, so he made sure to loop it all day. Even at home that night, the beat played on. When he woke the next morning, the words echoed endlessly as if they'd continued to do so, unbroken, throughout every second of his uneasy sleep.

Those three syllables drove young Braden to distraction. MIND THE GAP. It seemed too emphatic a warning to refer only to the railway platform, and his brain had instinctively recognized and internalized its grave import, so what *else* might it be cautioning against? Mum repeatedly assured him it was merely an admonishment for passengers to be careful boarding trains, but the more he thought about it, the more relevant it seemed. There were gaps everywhere, after all: beneath his bed, under all doors, separating the grins of gutter grates, between bookcases and school desks, opening up the undersides of bridges, beneath the boards of his home's porch and all its floors, between even the buttons and zippers of his clothes. He had a bad night when he realized that they were also in *people*—and so, of course, in *him*: between his fingers and toes, between his teeth, his nostrils, ears, and mouth were gaps, even his *butt*.

Mum sighed and begged him not to think so much about it. Dad made a joke about something called "existentialism" that Braden didn't understand and Mum didn't appreciate. But the rhythm of the words had become a part of his mental soundtrack, and everywhere he went, he walked to the beat: *mind the gap, mind the gap, mind the gap.* He even said it aloud a few times when he wasn't paying attention to what he was doing—which was increasingly often—and his friends called him weird until they stopped talking to him altogether. His lack of understanding bothered him day and night because he had a gap in his knowledge now, one he couldn't escape, but he could avoid other, more obvious iterations of emptiness. He refused to step over sewer grates and had to be carried up steps and stairs that weren't enclosed; lifts were absolutely out of the question. He wouldn't go near a door unless it was open, and only then if he could see what lay beyond it. He had his first full-blown panic attack when he passed a clothing store and looked up to see its name written in huge letters across its face: THE GAP.

His parents were at a loss, his doctors, too. They tried everything to convince him to stop picking away at this strange obsession, but he told them if he did, that absence would itself leave a gap, and *then* what? His schoolwork suffered and he had to be taken out of public education, not least because puberty was now falling upon him and his peers' uneducated mutterings about girl parts gave him a peculiar obsession with vaginas. Unlike his former friends, Braden seemed less interested in putting bits of himself into them and more hypnotically terrified by the unspeakable possibilities that lurked within. He got over this phase when his flustered parents sat him down and explained just how these intimate places worked in graphic detail; he understood then that they were not gaps as such but enclosed, finite, predictable spaces. He put these things in the same context as his own hidden hole, channels for life's matter to either enter or leave, and his fear of orifices was wiped away.

Encouraged by this success, Mum and Dad applied similar reasoning to other objects of terror… but the process broke down quickly. After all, one could never be *entirely* sure what lay beneath a bed or behind a door. The variations were infinite, as opposed to the anatomical certainty of a female body. And so, it seemed, were the gaps themselves. Even in so-called safe spaces, among the invisible cell-structures of the air, there might be millions or billions of tiny, unseen bacteria… so what else was lurking in each and every place where something more knowable was not?

All this worrying wore poor Braden down, and he started to develop health issues that became worse in young adulthood. A profound blow fell when some snide internet troll became aware of his condition and pointed out the existence of atomic spacing. The knowledge that even the *atoms* had gaps between them—that every human body was, in fact, 99.9999999% empty space—drove Braden to Lovecraftian levels of existential insanity that only strong neuroleptic medications could manage. He spent most of his time in a bed mounted on a solid wooden block, his walls unbroken swatches of plain color, his room empty of almost any decoration because he had decided that one large gap was perhaps slightly less terrifying than hundreds of tiny ones. His parents fretted and sent him to specialist after specialist, but his path seemed predetermined. Braden sickened, he ailed. And his body began to fail.

When the heart palpitations began, Braden realized what the message had been trying to tell him all along. MIND THE GAP was a clear warning of the pauses between heartbeats, for each split-second silence could yawn wider and wider until it swallowed him whole. A new rhythm took over his thoughts: instead of the three-beats-one-rest of *mind the gap,* finally retired after years of airplay, now it was the two-beats-one-rest feel of his internal metronome. The length of that rest varied from measure to measure, the percussive thud of his chest pump, and this uncertain timekeeping only added to his sense of dismay because he never quite knew what to expect. All he could do was lie awake and listen to his heartbeat and hope that it would continue into another bar after each rest, knowing that one day the gap would expand so wide that he couldn't help but fall into it, and that would be it for him. He would die and be cast into a gap in the earth, where worms wriggled through the empty spaces between dirt that only pretended to grit against itself, and there would be a new gap in the world where Braden had once stood and sat and slept and laughed and lived.

He began to insist upon cremation. Maybe that would end this infernal obsession—but though it was invisible to the naked eye, each grain of ash had the slightest gap between itself and its fellows, like any other atomic mass. Energy could not be created or destroyed; it merely took on new forms, so nothing ever ceased to be. It simply broke into more and more pieces, smaller and smaller and smaller, allowing the gaps to grow wider with every second. There was no escaping the emptiness for any living being or tiny cell or infinitesimal matter; in time, all would fall into the Nothing. Already the universe was practically infinite and yet every star, planet, and asteroid combined into a single mass would take up the tiniest speck of space… as if *that* were not bad enough, its endless emptiness was further shot through with the deeper greed of black holes. Existence itself was fatally fractured, for with every second—its temporal pulse broken apart from its siblings by mandated but secretly palpitating spaces like the failing heartbeat of a sick universe—every single atom in existence was already traveling through the void. Surrounded by the infinite gap. Devoured by it.

This, then, was the ultimate truth of the warning. MIND THE GAP, for it is all around us. It *is* us. It is nothing and it is everything.

Braden's mother was almost relieved when she walked into his room one morning and found that her poor, tormented young man had expired during the night. Peace had come for his anguished soul, at last. Though you wouldn't know it from the way his mouth yawned open like an abyss, as if at last, her troubled son had faced the god of all gaps and tried to swallow it into himself, or perhaps purge it from within with a silent scream, finally realising it had been within him all along.

Matthew R. Davis is a Shirley Jackson Award-nominated author and musician from Adelaide, South Australia, with over one hundred short stories and seven books published thus far. His latest books are the Aurealis Award-nominated horror collection Songs of Shadow, Words of Woe (JournalStone, 2025) and the non-fiction volume The Cure On Track: Every Album, Every Song (Sonicbond Publishing, 2025), with an indie film novelisation, a novella, and a novel due out in 2026. He lives with the award-winning artist Meg Wright (Red Wallflower) and her cats Juniper and Lexi.

Find out more at matthewrdavisfiction.wordpress.com.

Future in Flames Series: Cell Phones 4 U, Oil on Canvas

by Mel Harlan

Helen noticed the painter while parking for her shift. She'd only registered him because he wasn't rushing to work that morning, unlike the rest of Houston. He'd been fixed to the sidewalk with his easel—next to the roaring frontage road—utterly focused on his canvas in a way Helen vaguely admired; as much as she could with the half-notice of the hurried. She didn't say hello as she shoved her itchy polo into her too-tight khakis, popped Nicorette in her mouth to chew once and store by her back teeth, tacked on her name tag, and finger-combed her hair into a semblance of tidiness. Sweat threatened her forehead as she crossed the parking lot to Cell Phones 4 U.

Already propped up on the sidewalk was the sign with today's promotion, "40% off to the first 4 customers. A May the 4th miracle!" Helen entered to the familiar sound of the automated doorbell ringing and the generator running. Another storm knocked the power out all over town—for the third time this summer—and she was grateful for air conditioning. The cool air battled the store's signature smell of plastic, old feet (it'd been a shoe store some years before), and discarded dreams. The bare white walls were slotted with built-in racks of cell phones. Anything a luddite could want.

Her newest coworker, who'd only started this summer, awaited her behind the counter. He must be a student somewhere; he didn't have the shine wiped off him yet. Life hadn't chewed him up, swallowed, and then decided he wasn't a hefty enough meal before spitting him back out again. She knew by how he eager-beaver smiled at her, with his chiclet teeth, and his hands on his hips; a good little manager who took the tired backroom motivational posters shouting "COLLABORATE" and "TEAMWORK" to heart.

"Morning, Helen!" he greeted in an outfit that matched hers, minus the wrinkles. There was nothing wrong with... (she looked at his nametag to confirm) ...Chet. Helen just didn't want to remember him. Remembering meant she was coming back tomorrow, where he'd still be there to "MOTIVATE" her, since *he'd* earned the keys to open despite her greater tenure and age. She had at least twenty years on him.

"New phones came in," Chet said with mock disappointment. "Guess we have to put them out." He didn't say anything plainly; he spoke with the emphasis of a handbook-mandated welcome.

"As long as it's not during the rush," Helen said. Other than the painter, the parking lot was empty.

She placed her purse underneath the register counter instead of the back "team room." That room was even more lifeless. At least this one had windows.

"Greg says the inventory should go out by this afternoon," Chet said. Of course, he'd already spoken to their boss, who also moonlighted as the building's landlord. They were probably pickleball buddies.

"We can make a game of it." He used these games to muster motivation, for her as well as himself. Chet devised the activity: stock as many shelves of new inventory as you could in twenty minutes. Helen jumped as Chet yelled "Go!" While he still thought this job was temporary, like she had at first, he was flagging at doing a good job rather than simply doing the job.

And I'd let the job do me, Helen thought with an internal laugh.

As Chet tore into the shipping box of new cell phones and stocked them haphazardly at a frenetic pace, Helen began at a measured pace. She stationed herself so she could see the painter out of the corner of her eye. As she kneeled at her selected display case, her front pocket lighter dug into her hip, and the carpet's smell reached her. Underneath the current smell of plastic, all those bare feet on the carpet had seeped in, creating layers of smell where nothing ever came out. She could taste it in the back of her throat near her stashed Nicorette gum. Its peppery tingle helped block the smell—but not entirely.

She unlocked the cabinet and yanked open the box with her fingers. When she bent to reach further into the box, her gray, frizzed ponytail fell in her face. It was youthfully long since she refused to cut it short like all the other women her age. Instead, she tossed it back and began placing one package after another onto the shelves. They were so light she wondered if they were actually empty. Decoys to keep her "DEDICATED" to her "PRODUCTIVITY."

She lulled herself with the repetition as she wondered what the man was painting. Who would choose here to paint, of all places? She had a notion that she might travel to paint scenes of nature—something she'd never done or considered before.

While she stocked, she remained conscious of the painter's position, from his place on the sidewalk to the movement of his body. She mirrored him. He painted a stroke, she shelved one package. He glanced at the building, she glanced away. He paused, she paused. Helen preferred this game to Chet's.

"Time!" Chet called. He shuffled over huffing, his blue polo tightening and loosening around his belly. An inkblot of sweat darkened his center. "I got two boxes. You?"

"You win," Helen said coolly while continuing her slow unpacking.

"I said 'time'," Chet said in a half-exasperated way that made Helen want to smirk. When he saw her progress, he pronounced, "Well done, Helen!" like she didn't still have a half-full box.

She checked her watch. "I'm going to take my break."

"Helen, there's still an entire–"

She was already exiting the store, pulled toward the painter. Closer, she could see he was older than her, more solid than she expected for a painter. She expected someone daintier, with long, precise fingers that draped over the canvas. Not someone who looked like he should be down at the docks, hauling nets out of the water with his bare hands. His thick fingers were precise as they laid stroke after stroke of fresh paint. His jacket, which she'd thought was a windbreaker, was actually a rain slicker despite the clear sky and unforecasted rain.

Helen knew customers and he wasn't one. He didn't need help, didn't need to blame anyone. She had the perplexing feeling that she was superfluous. That, even though she came here every day, the painter was the only one meant to be here.

"How long do you plan on being here?" Helen yelled over the unending sound of cars braking and revving and billowing down the highway.

The painter finally looked at her. His gaze was uncomfortable, as weighty and worn as the rest of him. Like he was the one behind the counter and she was the one who needed something.

"As long as it takes." He didn't raise his voice, but she heard him clearly. It didn't cut through the din; it somehow suppressed it. He smiled briefly—as if he knew everything she was wondering—and she was surprised to see perfectly even, white teeth. One tooth was a little crooked, but it made him feel approachable.

"What are you painting?" she asked.

"The future," the painter replied.

"The future?" Helen repeated slowly.

"We see the world as it is, not as it could be," the painter replied. He looked at her again and her stomach fell, like someone jumped precisely at the right moment for her apartment elevator to drop. She checked to make sure her bowels hadn't splattered on the concrete.

"Huh," Helen said. She should have known he'd be a loony. Except those teeth said he didn't need money. Those teeth said *look and find out what's beyond the curtain, dear one.*

Over his shoulder, she saw the painting was of their shop. The squat, uninspired building had never been renovated and was a lot like the 80s. All tacky and sticky, a design aesthetic that would make hairspray proud. Their store sat between a boba shop and a chain store no one remembered. He'd gotten the bricks right, the tumble of litter by the gutter, and the signage—burned out with the '4' slanted to the right. Nothing abstracted or left to the imagination.

It was a perfectly captured moment—like a camera still—but she couldn't figure out *when* it was. It was the first thing that really mattered to Helen all week, maybe all year. Life was all about timing, when something either happened or it didn't. Her high hopes—the right schools, right connections—hadn't come to fruition, hadn't been timed correctly given the housing crisis and stock market crashes. So given how well everything was depicted, what time was it in the painting? It was supposed to be today—

the sign had today's promotion—except in the painting, it was leaning against the front window.

The second thing that wasn't right was the sky. It should have been light blue, but it was dyed dark purple. She couldn't tell if it was from the time of day or the smoke because of the third thing that was entirely wrong. The top of the building was in flames.

The more she stared at those fiery paint strokes, the more they seemed to flicker in motion. *A trick of the eye, surely?* An odd blink, a stray ray of sun would explain it. Not only could she see it, but she could hear it. The flames crackled and popped. It sounded like the Rice Krispies she'd had for breakfast. *Probably the wind.*

The vision sharpened and deepened the longer she stared. She could picture the inside of the store, which wasn't on the canvas. Cell phones melted in their packages. *The register sprung open under the heat and the bills burned and burned.*

The more she saw it, the more she wanted it to happen. She wasn't sure if she wanted the store to truly burn, or if she wanted the timing to be fulfilled. The thought made her grasp for a falter in the illusion until she found one. "Flames should be coming out of the windows," Helen informed him and her own voice broke the painting's spell.

He continued adding more layers of color to the roof.

"Are the windows next?" Helen prompted. When he didn't answer, she tried, "Is it for sale?" She could tell it wasn't, but couldn't help herself from asking. She wanted to see it finished and save it for herself.

"Thrice questioned and thrice answered," replied the painter. "You are out of questions." The painter's eyes stared through her. If she tried, she'd never be able to recall the color; she'd been too busy feeling their intensity.

Helen glanced at her watch and was surprised her break was already over. As she hurried across the parking lot—late again—the highway roar and heat were already returning. She hadn't noticed it, but she hadn't been sweating at all despite the full morning sun.

She called back, "My coworker might call the cops for loitering."

The painter was unmoved.

"Yeah, I know. He's a cock. But I won't be able to talk him out of it. In case you need to mosey elsewhere."

The front door chimed as she entered. The boxes were gone, Chet must have already put away the new inventory. She'd hoped for a slight breeze from the air conditioning, but was hit with an unpleasant warmth instead. "Generator off again?"

Chet announced, "We're supporting profitability! And, as a bonus, Greg will turn it back on when we make a sale." His words were jaunty, but his polo was already darkening with sweat.

*

Helen sat at the counter while Chet waited at the front window. While they were both on shift, he preferred Helen to 'guard' the register while he stationed himself by the door to take walk-ins. It reminded her of stationing a hippo next to a watering hole. No takers.

The store was silent with the generator "turned off." What Chet didn't mention was that Greg didn't want to pay to refuel the diesel. Two perfectly fine, perfectly empty, jerry cans sat unused in the back room. Like any frugal boss, he'd planned for this scenario. Rather than ensuring it was running, he'd made sure their register ran on rechargeable batteries, which charged underneath the counter. The sunlight, instead of their fluorescents, was free until sundown (when they'd already be closed).

It didn't take long before Chet said, "We'll never get a walk-in with that guy out there. He's scaring people."

Helen's top lip frosted with sweat. "He's not hurting anyone. Just painting."

"Greg wouldn't like it."

Helen shrugged. "If they're too scared to be in a strip mall with vagrants, they should shop elsewhere."

"Really, Helen?" Chet shook his head before calling Greg, who quickly agreed. Chet gave her an 'I told you so' expression. Helen didn't hate him for this; hate required energy. She simply shrugged and waited for the next move Greg would require of him.

Next, Chet called the police. While they waited for their arrival, a small rainstorm came and went. Helen worried the painter might leave, until she realized he'd been prepared. It only disturbed him long enough to put up his rainslicker's hood.

Two hours later, a squad car pulled in.

"Mind the register," Chet said to Helen as he met them outside.

Helen wandered to the front window and crossed her arms. She wished she could read lips. "Move it along," she murmured to herself, narrating the scene as the cops raised their hands to the painter. "You can't loiter. If you stay, we'll be forced to give you a ticket."

"I see the future. I can do what I want," Helen parroted in high falsetto and felt better. She couldn't take anything about the painter or his painting seriously if he had that voice. "Thrice ye... thrice!" She couldn't remember exactly what he said and sang instead, "Thrice, thrice, thrice!"

She lost the energy to mock the painter as she and the store baked from the sunny windows. Her thoughts returned to the fire. She didn't need to imagine the heat, she could already feel it, but she tried to envision the flames licking the walls. The crackle as plastic shrank and warped and snapped. She frowned, unable to conjure the same vividness the painting had stirred.

"How had it started? Maybe the fire would be electrical?" Helen mused. The building certainly had old enough wiring. "Or a lightning strike? Don't those cause fires?" She wasn't sure.

What if there really was a fire? She didn't believe the painter knew the future—*of course not, no one could know the future even if he happened to have a rain slicker when he needed it*—but maybe he could envision one where the building was on fire. How many windows would break? Would it be so hot that it burned blue? She remembered that one fact from science class. The hotter the fire, the deeper the color it burned. And it would burn. There were no sprinklers. While the fire department insisted, she knew Greg had disconnected them. For profitability.

In that case, would Greg send her to another one of his businesses?

"No. He already has those staffed," Helen murmured.

And there'd be plenty of bills to pay to deal with afterwards. Insurance only covered so much, and he might need to pay some out of pocket. Certainly more to worry about than Helen's job. She'd be simply another loss.

"Would they rebuild a strip mall here?" No, she didn't think so. Probably a Target. And that would be nice enough for Helen who could meander those aisles for hours. She hadn't figured out what she wanted to be—she couldn't see it—and the shelves were full of inspiration. You never knew what you might find.

She placed her hand on the hot windowpane as the cops gestured for the painter to turn around. He did. They cuffed him before helping him duck into the car's back seat. They shoved his painting into the trunk.

Let him finish, Helen thought helplessly. She'd learned a long time ago that no one really listened to her. Not her cat. Or customers. Or Chet. She was a ghost, haunting somewhere she should no longer be.

Chet strode into the shop. His bird chest was so high she thought it might snap.

"Where are they taking him?" Helen asked before Chet could tell her what she'd witnessed. She couldn't remember the last time she'd asked anything of him.

He marched behind the counter. "Wherever he wants to go. They'll drop him off with a warning."

Helen hoped he'd leave custody and come back to finish the painting. Unless he'd finished it? *Then he'd never be back.* Her Nicorette bumped a small ulcer and she winced.

As Chet grabbed his phone, Helen couldn't resist asking. "Did you see the painting?"

"Painting?" Chet said as he dialed.

"Yeah, the painting," Helen said with exasperation.

"What about it?" Chet held the phone to his ear.

"Was it done?" Helen wasn't sure which answer she wanted.

Chet shrugged. "I don't know art. It's all 'up to interpretation'." He used air quotes then and she remembered—Chet was an idiot. "Can't wait to let Greg know!"

"Maybe he'll promote you," Helen said dourly. Chet didn't notice her tone, he was too proud of himself.

"Maybe!" Chet replied.

He held up a finger as she heard Greg come on the line. Within a few moments, Chet announced, "Greg approves!" with cold-brew breath and hung up.

"Chet," Helen said and then regretted it. He looked so hopeful. "It's my break." It was too early for her tuna salad sandwich, and she wasn't hungry, but she grabbed her purse anyway and headed out back. From her bag, she pulled out her latest brand of cigarettes. Every week she tried a new pack. This week's was KOOL Super Longs. The blue box had caught her eye and looked like peppermint gum. She didn't love them so far, but had started smoking for more mandated breaks. That the menthol helped deaden the store's scent also helped.

She passed through the team room where the dreadful poloed man glared at her from the poster that announced *If you can see it, you can be it!* There was something about the smiling employee with their thumbs up. Maybe it was his too-white teeth that were so bright, they looked like veneers. *Something you could see in the dark.* Or maybe it was the way he looked too excited about his polo-wearing existence. Her own itched enough that if she acknowledged it, it would be all she could think about. As she exited, Helen noticed another set of inventory boxes that Chet had missed, and a smirk bloomed.

Helen decided to give the painter until closing to come back. If he wasn't finished, she could see it then. She hungered to see it, needed to see it completed. She couldn't handle this too remaining unfinished. If he didn't return, would she take up painting and complete her own version?

That won't be necessary. He'll be back, Helen reassured herself.

✱

"It's about that time," Chet called from the front of the store.

The entire day had dragged along, especially without any visitors. The boba shop had closed early, leaving most to drive up and drive by, if they considered stopping at all. The chain store could be closed or open, she wasn't sure which since no one visited except seniors. None today.

Inside the store, the heat had slowed time to a crawl. An aching crawl to closing time, without the benefit of alcohol, unlike the Semisonic song Chet was playing as part of his end-of-day routine. She was grateful for the lighter digging into her hip, all hour, every hour, which kept her awake. Her usual trick to prevent Chet from sending sleeping photos of her to Greg.

"Closing time," Helen said in disbelief.

"Closing time," Chet echoed in song as he locked the register for the day.

Helen snatched her purse and headed to her car. The front door dinged its mournful call after her.

"Have a nice night," Chet yelled after her, affronted.

Helen spat out her gum, got in her car, started the engine, and waited. *The painter was running late,* she promised herself. She sat with the windows rolled slightly down, enough for a breeze rather than a cigarette. She didn't need one outside of work, that habit was relegated to the property. Her own vehicle lacked any smell since her pine air freshener baked out years ago.

As Chet locked up for the night, he set the sign against the front window, surprised out of his order of operations since she usually let him walk her to her car. Another "good manager" deed for his day since his car was parked in back. He was mumbling to himself, likely saying something like *if she gets mugged, it's her own fault.* He was so young, he still took work personally.

After removing his key, Chet pulled the door handle to make sure it was locked and stomped to his car. No one parked in back if they could help it. Technically, Helen was supposed to park there as an employee, but always refused. It was the one rule Chet didn't like to follow either; he wouldn't even go there on his break because of the dumpster's wafting stench.

He drove away in his gifted vehicle. His parents had given him their old car, a sedan with a wonky, wobbling engine and a burned-out headlight. Neither of which Chet had bothered to replace all summer, even if he could have replaced his own headlight on their hourly wage. Helen couldn't imagine the privilege. Her own father had died a penniless artist while she'd been in college studying economics.

Eventually, the sky darkened and it was after hours for all the stores. Two workers exited the big box store, arm in arm. They high-fived each other and kissed. Helen wondered how they'd managed to amuse themselves all day, alone in an empty store. Then they drove away, leaving Helen alone in the lot. The May the 4th sign was barely legible until the outside lights kicked on for the night. LED bulbs cast the parking lot in stark relief. It brightened while draining color from the world, like being in an ill-lit sci-fi flick.

Another hour passed and Helen considered going home. The idea flickered and went out like a faulty candle, extinguished by the idea of missing the painter by moments. She'd already been waiting hours. What were a few more? *In for a penny, in for a pound.* The same logic had already kept her at Cell Phones 4 U four years too long.

It was getting late when a car appeared. The headlights blinded her and she blinked away the spots in her eyes. Her heart crashed forward, ready to greet the painter, when she realized she'd been blinded by one headlight instead of two. Chet. He passed her and turned down the alley to the strip mall back lot.

"Oh, Chet," Helen said sadly as he parked in the back. She wouldn't have guessed Chet would set the fire, but she could imagine it now—even if it was an accident—since he'd likely been asked to refill the generator. Greg had heard about the lack of customers and decided to refill it to catch someone escaping the heat.

It didn't take long before Chet was leaving again, his one headlight leading the way. It was faster than she'd predicted, fast enough to be careless, and it would be this act that would burn the building down. She waited a few minutes, but was disappointed. No flames. Not even smoke. She was sure now that the painter wasn't coming back. Somewhere between dusk and Chet, she'd decided that was all she'd get. But the fire—she knew where that would be.

Because it has to be today. Tomorrow, Chet would remember to put the sign away. And that meant the building would still be there and the timing would *never* be right.

He could have lit something. He could have. It might be starting slowly, to tempt her to go inside and see. Helen squeezed the steering wheel until her knuckles turned white. If that was true, she had to know. She had to be sure.

Helen drove around back, parked, and crawled out of the seat. Her legs ached as they stretched for the first time in hours. The dumpster smell reached her immediately, refreshingly honest like the old puddle in the middle of the lot. While she didn't have keys anymore, that privilege had been lost years ago when she'd forgotten to open, she was counting on Chet's unavoidable forgetfulness.

He'll have been too worried about the standby generator to remember the lock, she thought. *Especially since it's running.* He'll have reminded himself of all his steps. Make sure generator is off. Open cap. Get gas can ready. Pour. Turn on and make sure it's working. Sometimes it gave a little extra kick, which forced the automatic shutoff. He'd have to try starting it again and he'd be so busy not forgetting how to do it perfectly that he'd have forgotten how to do the entire job.

There was no one around, despite the bustling highway traffic that never died. Normally, especially as a woman alone at night, Helen would have been really worried about something happening to her—Houston had plenty of car thieves and parking lot assaults—but it wouldn't matter if the back door was unlocked. If it was unlocked, then she could see the fire starting. She grabbed the handle and it was still warm from the remembered daytime. She didn't look around to avoid looking suspicious; she was simply another employee, in her uniform, doing what all employees do. Going to work.

She pulled and, for a moment, it stuck. In that second, Helen's heart thumped so loudly she forgot she wasn't supposed to be there. Another second longer, of her full weight behind her arm pulling on the door, and it popped free with a screech.

He'd left it unlocked! Helen smiled for the first time that day —a brief flash of polished crooked teeth—and entered the back room. No alarm sounded. Greg had canceled that bill too.

The place was dark. She almost touched the light switch before realizing it would announce to the world she was inside. Not to mention, the painting didn't show the lights on. Her hand fell away and her eyes adjusted the blackness to shades of gray.

As expected, both gas cans were by the back door. In the daylight, they were bright, fire engine red. Now, they were merely gray. She glanced around and even ducked into the front. No fire anywhere. Only the acrid smell of diesel.

On the surface, she couldn't believe it. But her logical self agreed: Chet didn't have anything—other than the generator itself—that would cause a spark. Not to mention, he wanted to be good at this job while it lasted. That same part had understood what the painter had awoken, had wrestled with possibilities all day, had convinced her to be here.

Disappointment, an emotion she hadn't felt in years, filled the back of her throat. She'd wanted the painting to be true and, more than that, she'd fully expected it to be. Time was short with only six hours until sunrise. Another two until Chet opened. What were the chances that a storm would strike? Or for the electrical to short-circuit? As the timing narrowed, so did the range of possibilities.

She turned to leave and then stopped under the poster's regard. In the dark, the employee had become a disembodied smile hovering like a Cheshire cat. Only the suggestion of a person. On his left, as bright as his teeth, was the ever-present *If you can see it, you can be it!*

Helen pivoted and approached the gas as if it were a mirage. With each step, it didn't fade or disappear. She grabbed the first one's cold plastic handle and hefted it. Too light. She shook it to make sure it was empty. The other one wouldn't be, though. Chet would have saved the other for their shift, so he didn't have to sweat through his polo again. The second was heavier, but not too heavy. She held it aloft and paused. No one appeared like they did in the movies to yell "freeze."

From her front pocket, her lighter was an unspoken promise. The carpet would be tinder from all the polyester fibers. The walls were moldering kindling. Like her air freshener, the plastic would smell more at first as it burned, perfuming the air with its shrieks. Then the smell would burn away, removed as the carpet would be cleansed by flame, until even the old foot smell was gone. It'd burn to scentless dust, that would never coat the back of her throat again.

The break room would alight. The back door would splinter. The poster would burn and blacken and fall. It would all permanently burn.

She pulled the lighter from her pocket. Her hip throbbed its final goodbye before it relaxed in relief. *I will see it, I will see it*, Helen thought and began.

Mel Harlan is a consultant and writer. She created the series she always wanted to read with the Jack Anderson novels. Her short fiction has appeared or is forthcoming in Allegory, Creepy Podcast, Foofaraw Press, Graveside Press, and Thirteen Podcast.

She lives in Houston, TX with her husband. When not writing, she is probably searching for the perfect latte.

Lifeline
by Julia LaFond

Content warnings: death, gambling

In the studio waiting room, the silence broken only by the buzzing lights and my ringing ears, it was harder to pretend this was just a game. Or to be more accurate, that there wasn't anything riding on it. In the first round I could focus on the computer screen in front of me and pretend the numbers going up, up, and further up were points, not thousands of dollars. But now that I had a second to breathe, it was harder. Somehow, my knowledge of obscure history had won me more money than I could make in a lifetime of waiting tables.

Rubbing my temples, I told myself that this was just an unusually elaborate Trivia Club session. I forced myself to believe the only thing on the line was a bucket of poker chips so I didn't lose it (literally *and* figuratively) in the impending final round.

The door clicked open, and someone finally came to get me. His tailored black suit made me keenly aware of how worn my blue ruffled skirt was. I smoothed it down, quietly hoping no one would notice the grease stains my blouse couldn't quite cover up. If I won—no, if I *were* to *coincidentally* win—the lottery today, I should ask where he went shopping.

He led me to a shiny chrome podium to the left of two occupied ones. Next to me was a man with tanned skin and short brown hair who continuously fiddled with his clip-on bowtie. Beyond him was a 20-something woman with short blonde hair and a pantsuit so fancy I wondered why she bothered auditioning. Then again, you can never tell—maybe she just got lucky at the thrift store.

Against my better judgment, I snuck a glance at the audience. The seats, however, were empty, and I breathed a sigh of relief. Being filmed was bad enough; a live audience would have sent me running for the hills.

"Greetings, contestants!"

I spun back around to see a gentleman I couldn't quite think of as elderly. He had balding gray hair and his pale skin was wrinkled, but something about his smiling eyes made him seem much younger. One thing was for sure: only a game show host would wear a purple velvet suit, let alone pull it off. This really was the final "mystery" round.

"Congratulations to all three of you!" he continued, looking at each of us in turn. "Believe me when I say, you *earned* your place on this stage. Haven't they?" He turned to wink at the camera.

His delivery was so hammy, I had to cover my mouth to stifle a laugh, my nerves utterly gone. It was impossible to take this seriously when our host so clearly wasn't.

"How about some introductions?"

The other two turned out to be Casey, a plumber from Idaho, and Lacey, a media consultant from the Big Apple.

"Now then," said our host, rubbing his hands, "I should explain the new rules."

Casey and I shot each other a confused glance because our host completely skipped over introducing himself. Considering he was soaking up enough limelight to power the US electrical grid, that was strange. Then again, maybe he assumed we already knew who he was. Sort of like how no one bothered to tell us the name of the game show.

My stomach roiled as I realized not even the fliers advertising auditions said *which* game show it was for. I'd meant to ask, but there hadn't been any time to. Maybe that was intentional.

"Now that we've made it past the money round," the host continued, oblivious to our disquiet, "you have the option to cash out your winnings—as well as your lifeline penalties."

I flinched, wondering what the penalty was. They'd made it clear using any of our three lifelines would reduce our score, so I'd planned not to. But the hint-dispensing button had hovered invitingly at the edge of the screen, and I couldn't quite remember whether I'd succumbed to temptation in the heat of the moment.

"Now let's reveal today's penalty!" A recorded drumroll echoed through the studio as he pulled a slip of paper from his pocket. "Ten years off your lifespan!"

I really did laugh this time, but after a joke like that, I was probably supposed to. Casey joined in, though there was a nervous edge to his chuckles. Lacey folded her arms and pursed her lips, waiting for him to tell us the actual rules.

He turned to beam at me. "Now that's the confidence we love to see! It's true, in the life round, you'll have the chance to earn much more than that! But if your score drops too low, you'll lose your earnings *and* still have the penalties to pay." He scanned all three of us, still smiling, but with a gravity that sent chills down my spine. "If you want to cut your losses, this is your last chance."

"Enough!" snapped Lacey. "This is absurd! Edit this out in post and tell us the rules already!"

"I have."

My skin prickled at his sincerity. It wasn't possible, but he certainly seemed to believe what he was saying. I wished I could remember whether I'd used my lifelines—if I hadn't, I needed to leave right now. But if I had, was any amount of money worth ten years off my life, let alone twenty or thirty?

I shook my head. It was just a joke. It *had* to be a joke. Which meant there was no reason to walk away.

"Fine, then," Lacey snorted. "If you're going to be like that, I *will* cash out."

"Are you sure?" For the first time, the host's smile faded. "You won't get a chance to recoup the lifeline you used."

"Positive!" She turned to look at Casey and me, eyes full of contempt. "Word of advice: you should too. This is obviously some sort of scam." She flounced off the stage, waving without looking back. "Don't say I didn't warn—"

Clutching her chest, she toppled to the floor. The employees sprang into action, loading her onto a waiting stretcher.

A *waiting* stretcher.

"Are you going to kill us if we try to leave?" I blurted out, trying to understand what was happening. "Did you poison us, or—"

"No, no, no!" Our host made an X with his arms. "In fact, we'll make sure she goes straight to the hospital. But it looks like ten years was more than she had left. Bad for her, good for her beneficiary!" He cleared his throat. "Now then —do either of you want to cash out?"

Casey shook his head frantically, and I wondered how many lifelines he'd used. More than that, I wondered how many I'd used in my quiz-induced fugue state.

"And you, ma'am?"

Taking a deep breath, I dug my nails into my palms. This wasn't real. It couldn't be real. It was an elaborate session of Trivia Club—one I was going to win.

"I'll stay."

With a satisfied smile, our host pressed a button; our podiums hummed to life. "Right then! The final round has two phases. For the first phase, aside from playing for years, the rules are the same as the last round: right answers make your score go up, a string of right answers multiplies your score, wrong answers break combos and reduce your score, and you're out if you hit zero. Also, if you have any lifelines left, you *can* still use them."

A pop-up informed me I still had all three. It took all my self-control not to smash the screen and storm out.

"Now let's get started!"

The first question popped up, and I slipped back into a state of flow. Nothing could rattle me—not the camera crew, not our strange host, and not even the fact that the latest quiz was about my personal history. My maternal grandmother's maiden name, the day of the week I adopted my first cat, how long it had been since I kissed anyone. I answered question after question, entirely focused on getting a perfect combo no matter what. My score went up, up, and further up.

"That's the round!"

With a gasp, I looked up, dazed to find myself standing in the middle of the studio. The lights made my eyes water, but not even they could outshine our host's pearly smile.

"Let's take a look at the current scores, shall we?"

Behind him, a screen flickered to life: my earnings on the left, and Casey's on the right. My head buzzed at how high both my money and life scores were. I wouldn't need to work another day of what was going to be a very long life.

Except the round wasn't over.

My throat tightened up. Desperate for a distraction, I looked at Casey's score. He'd done almost as well as me on the first round, but on this round, not so much. Between the lifelines and a string of wrong answers, he'd barely avoided elimination with a net positive of ten years.

Our host chortled. "In the battle of the sexes, looks like women won this round! But no one got eliminated, so that leaves the final challenge."

Some of the employees wheeled in a bingo ball dispenser. It was so cheesy, my face flushed red. Gripping the podium, I resisted the strange urge to knock the cart over and smash the dispenser to pieces. As bizarre and infuriating as the entire situation was, I couldn't afford to lose my winnings by getting kicked off the show.

The host turned the crank. "For today's finale—"

One of the ping-pong balls fell into his waiting hand, and the drum roll played once again. The host squinted at it, eventually proclaiming, "Double or nothing!"

The screen lit up with a golden "2X" on one side and a bright red "0" on the other.

"For this challenge, one participant gets the chance to double their earnings with a single question! But if they're wrong, they lose it all! Though that *doesn't* apply to the lifeline penalties—win or lose, that's ten years per lifeline you gotta pay back."

Casey's breath hissed in, and he swayed on his feet. He'd used all three lifelines. If he lost, it was thirty years down the drain without a single cent to show for it. Though I'd hate to lose now, I, at least, hadn't used any—

My eyes strayed down to my screen, and with a start, I realized I had, in fact, used all my lifelines to preserve my perfect combo. Letting myself get so immersed had backfired spectacularly.

"When I say *one*," the host boomed, "I mean *one*. Exactly one of you gets to play this final round." He sauntered over to me. "The leading contestant gets first pick! Would you like to Double or Nothing?"

With more money and years than I knew what to do with, the answer was obvious. "No, thank you!"

He leaned in, getting right up in my face. "Are you *sure*?"

Unable to stand the intensity of his megawatt smile, I looked away, only for Casey's gaze to pull me in. He folded his hands, quietly pleading with me. If I didn't accept, he'd have to. We both knew he'd choke, and then he might die in front of me like Lacey did.

"Actually," I sighed, cursing my soft heart, "I *would* like to. Final answer."

"Excellent!" Rubbing his hands, he darted over to Casey. "In that case, sir, thanks for playing! You had a good run, but let's give our finalist a clear stage!"

Casey gave me a quick nod before bolting for his life. The door clanged shut behind him, echoing through the oddly silent studio.

"Right then!" The host returned to the center of the stage. "Are you ready?"

My heart was racing and I'd never get the sweat stains out of my shirt, but if I waited any longer, I'd faint. "As I'll ever be," I croaked out.

"The final question is..."

The drumroll sounded one last time.

"On what day are you going to die?"

I almost laughed from relief, because the answer was staring me in the face. All I had to do was convert my winnings into a date. But when I looked back up, the words caught in my throat. Those years were supposed to be *added* to my lifespan, but I had no idea what the original number was. If I assumed average life expectancy, I could make a pretty good guess, but that's all it would ever be: a guess. Maybe I would have lived to 100, or maybe I would have died in a car accident tomorrow. How was I supposed to narrow it down to the day?

"I don't know," I mumbled, shaking my head.

The screen displayed "I don't know." I gasped at my stray words being counted as a guess.

"Is that your final answer?"

Something in his tone washed away every last scrap of optimistic denial my mind had stubbornly clung to. This man—with his *tacky* suit and his *smug* smile—had just made me bet thirty years of my life on a game I couldn't win. I should have listened to Lacey: this was a scam from the start.

But since I didn't have anything left to lose, I'd at least make him regret it.

"I don't know!" I shouted, kicking off my heels. "No one knows when they'll die!"

"Correct!"

I froze in place, my sleeves falling back down my arms. "What?"

"That's the correct answer!" He grinned broadly as the screen exploded into fireworks, my earnings doubling in size. "Congratulations on becoming our latest champion!"

Leaning against the podium, I gaped at the screen. This was the part where I was supposed to laugh and squeal and scream, but I couldn't bring myself to. I might have won, but Lacey was gone. She might have been a stuck-up snob, but she didn't deserve to die. And how many other people had lost their lives to this pointless game?

My rage finally overpowered my shock, and I unfastened my earrings, determined to give the host a well-deserved beating.

He clicked his tongue. "Now, now, don't be like that!"

I shoved past the podium.

"In that case, you'll get your check in the mail!"

Everything went dark. When I opened my eyes, I was back in my apartment. Which might have convinced me it was just a dream, if I weren't missing the heels I'd kicked off. But all I could do was wait to see if I'd really get any money.

When the check finally came, the attached note claimed my "poor sportsmanship" cost me my spot in the centennial championship. But getting out of it *that* easily sounded way too good to be true—kind of like the audition fliers I wish I'd ignored. Either way, it will be a hundred years before I find out whether I'll be forced to risk it all again.

Or maybe I'll die tomorrow. After all, nobody knows exactly how much time they have…

Julia LaFond got her master's in geoscience from Penn State University. She's had short stories published via venues such as Worlds of Possibility, PodCastle, and Night Frights, and she also writes TTRPG content under the brand Calenmir's RPGs. In her spare time, Julia enjoys reading and gaming.

Website: https://jklafondwriter.wordpress.com/

Gumball
by Michael Allen Rose

"Stop it, Ben!"

Ben's mother snatched the big green gumball from his pudgy, seven-year-old fingers, just before they deposited the sphere into his gaping mouth.

"Break it in half and share with your sister."

"Fine."

Fran aimed her eyes back at the road, as her son promptly placed the gumball back on his tongue and sneered at his older sister, Mary, across the back seat.

"Mom!" came Mary's cry, "Ben's not sharing!" Mary was ten and assured of her intellectual superiority.

"Am so." Ben burped.

"Stop it, Ben! That's disgusting! Now give half that gumball to your sister!"

"I don't want it anymore, mom. He spit all over it."

Fran rubbed her right temple with a temporarily free hand, and tried to figure out a way to escape. She wasn't used to being in a car with her children. It was like a prison camp on balding tires. Mark, her husband of twelve years, usually picked up the children from school in the afternoons, but today he had a meeting he had to attend.

Something about the price of beans in Brazil.

"You know, one of these days, you're going to choke on one of those damned things, and then what are you going to do?" Fran asked her offspring.

There was a moment of silence. Fran was excited about this not only for the sense of relief, but also because she had apparently gotten her children to think about the consequences of their actions. Perhaps this was a turning point!

"Mommy said a bad word!" Mary and Ben whooped with righteous glee.

As they repeated themselves in a duet of sing-song voices, many more expletives came to her mind, but her teeth were aware of this, and conspired to bite her tongue. She and Mark had decided long ago to curb their use of "vulgar" language in front of the children. The last thing they needed at thirty-something was to have one of the children tell them they had a "shitty day" in front of the grandparents.

Enough had been said about the fact that Ben and Mary were enrolled in public school.

"There's a lovely private school in Springfield that would be very good for the children. It's only half an hour away and it would be so much better for them." Her mother's words still echoed in her ears as if they were all in the car together. "You know, your father and I saw a report on the TV about public schools, and they are simply dens of sex and violence and dope these days. I don't know what the world is coming to anymore.

"It's not safe, like it was when we were young."

"Sure it was, mom." she said to the voices in her head.

Mary interrupted her thoughts. "Mom, Ben won't stay on his side of the car!"

"Ben, stay over on your side."

Ben grunted in reply, and Fran heard a slapping sound. Next, there was a soft whimpering.

"Oh, god, please no..." Fran thought to herself, but it was too late.

The whimpering slowly built to a soft cry, and then for a moment, all seemed to be quiet. She was reminded of a thunderstorm breaking, when Ben's bawling began to reverberate off the interior of the car.

"She hit me!" screamed Ben, as his mother tried to think of life before children.

"Mommy has to stop at the grocery store to pick up supper," said Fran, as she pulled into the parking lot of the local Jewel-Osco, "so I want you two to sit here and be good, okay? Don't open the doors for anybody and don't bother each other."

"Okay," came the unenthusiastic reply from the rear of the car.

"Can I have some pudding pops?" Ben inquired.

Fran denied the request with a look and unhitched the door keys from the ignition key. She wouldn't want to leave the kids in the car without any radio to occupy their minds. Lack of radio would assure that one or both of them would probably be bleeding from a fresh punch in the nose when she returned. Children, it seemed to her, had the attention span of a mayfly on speed. She left the car with a small noise that was intended to mean "I'll be back soon" and quickly took off toward the supermarket.

In the back seat of the car, the kids immediately started to get antsy. Ben decided that now would be the ideal time to pull out his second gumball. Ben was rarely without some sort of confection. His pockets were stuck shut fifty percent of the time. He didn't really care, as long as his stomach was happy, and his teeth had that lovely stinging sensation.

Sugar was his god.

It was a beautiful green gumball. Ben's friend Skip didn't like the green ones.

Skip said they were alien poop and tasted like somebody barfed up a watermelon.

Skip was a doofus. Ben placed the ball between his teeth, savoring the moment. He bit through only the tiniest fraction of the coating, and the flavor began to seep into his mouth, mixing with his saliva. Only seconds until green heaven. He felt a sharp crack on the back of his head.

"Mom said to share, Ben!" his sister screeched as her hand retreated from the back of his head. "That would teach him to be a selfish little poop eater," Mary thought to herself. She noticed Ben wasn't saying anything in reply. He was just sort of staring into thin air.

"I swallowed the gumball?" Ben's mind echoed with the words. "I swallowed my gumball! The magnificent green gumball that I paid twenty-five hard-earned cents for? I swallowed it?"

No, not quite. It was sort of halfway in between. A second, gumball-sized lump appeared right above his adam's apple. The next thing he knew, he realized he wasn't drawing much air into his lungs. It felt sort of tight, and he began to perspire a bit. Mary noticed that her little brother was turning slightly redder than usual.

"Are you okay, dork?" she inquired of her now uncomfortably shifting brother.

This was the nicest way she could bring herself to phrase the question, so she was a little irked when he didn't answer her. "I asked are you okay?"

Ben's face began to turn a bit bluish and he started to make little gasping noises.

He began to flail wildly around.

"Stop it! Stop it!" Mary screamed as Ben's arms swung around the back seat. "I'm going to tell mom!"

Ben looked at his sister, his eyes beginning to well up with tears. He pointed to his throat with a plump finger and made a sort of barking noise.

"Are you choking, Ben?" Mary felt the first inkling of concern come into her mind as she tried to decide what course of action to pursue. Ben was now turning a very noticeable shade of blue, eyes open wide with the first shades of panic.

"Gllllfff!" shrieked Ben, as he flailed desperately hoping to dislodge the gumball.

Mary stretched back her hand, and hesitating only a moment, did what she had to do to save her brother.

The punch sounded like a bass drum in the small car. She hit Ben in the chest with all her might. At that moment, the gumball came shooting from Ben's gullet like a bullet, smashing into the front windshield with a sharp crack. Throwing open the door, Ben breathed in a huge gulp of air, and promptly fell out of the car. He lay there on the parking lot pavement on his back, panting heavily, dizzy with strain. As the heat receded from his face, he looked up and saw that his sister was peering over the edge of the back seat, looking down at him. The clouds floating far above her face were regaining their normal colors.

"Are you okay?" Mary asked, a hint of distress in her voice.

Ben nodded the affirmative and grunted in response.

"Stupid. You had me worried. You should've listened to mom."

Ben picked himself up off the pavement and slowly crawled back into the car.

Looking around the lot, he saw that nobody had seen his blue-faced plunge from the automobile. Thank heaven for small miracles.

"I want my gumball back."

"Well, go get it, you little turd."

Obviously his sister was going to be of no help.

Ben began crawling over the gap between the front seats, looking toward the floor for his beloved green globe of sweetness. No choking episode was going to keep him from the sugary goodness he had been anticipating. Besides, a quarter was not that easy to come by in his experience, and he was going to get his money's worth.

He looked over his shoulder and saw his sister staring out the side window. She looked angry and he thought that perhaps now was not the best time to mention that his throat hurt. As he rotated his head back toward the front of the car, his vision passed over something odd. Ben looked up quickly to see if it had been a spider. Ben hated spiders.

His eyes focused on the anomaly, exactly where it had been when he first spied it. Well, it hadn't moved, so it surely wasn't a spider. He peered closer, nearly losing his balance.

It was much worse than a spider.

Mary looked up from her world watching to hear the howl of a banshee. Ben was crying again. "That's all little brothers are good for," she thought to herself. "What's the matter with you?" She followed his gaze to rest her vision upon a fractured portion of the front windshield about an inch in diameter. Tiny bits of green candy coating were etched into the crack in the windshield, and lines were radiating out from the central dent. Her stomach made a nervous sound.

Ben was wailing, gibbering something about being in trouble. Mary wouldn't be able to console him anyway, so she kept her mouth shut. They both instinctively looked toward the store to see if Fran was coming back yet, but there was no sign of her.

"We've got to fix it!" Mary attempted to scream over Ben's constant sobbing. She shoved her younger brother out of the way and dove toward the glove box, hitting her head on the dash. It didn't register in her nervousness. Opening the glove box sent maps and envelopes flying all over, and before she had a chance to worry about it, she was lying over the front seat, knocked out cold.

Ben had seen his sister hit the dash, but he hadn't expected this. He stopped crying immediately. What was the good if nobody was there to feel sorry for you? There were more important matters at hand. There was a crack in mommy's windshield, the contents of the glove compartment were spread liberally about the vehicle, his throat still hurt from his choking episode, and his older sister was passed out over the passenger seat, drooling on the roadmaps. Worst of all, that had been his last gumball.

Ben thought very hard about what he was going to do. He could run away, but his mom had a car, and he figured she'd probably be more likely to run him over than usual in the state she would be in when she saw the crack. He tried to think of a way to fix the fractured glass, but the only substance he could think of was bubble gum, and he was tired of bubble gum at this point. He thought about blaming it on a stranger, but... actually, that might work. What would he tell his mother? That a stranger had come up to the car and tried to get in? That would do it! In her state of panic over her children's safety, Fran wouldn't even notice the green candy dust around the crack's edges! Then he looked back at his sister.

Her chest was still moving, so he assumed she wasn't dead or anything. Perhaps if he could lift her back into her seat, she would wake up before their mother got back from her shopping trip. As he struggled to move Mary, he realized that his time spent on the couch eating candy and watching cartoons should have been scheduled around a healthy exercise regime. He could barely pick her up before she slumped back into the front seat. Thinking as quickly as possible, he jammed himself into the small floor space underneath his sister's head, and began to push.

Mary was dreaming. In her dream she was crossing a beautiful river. The current was gently lapping about her hips, and she felt the warm sand at the bottom of the stream between her toes. Some small, singing birds flew over her head, and she waved at them. It was a perfect world. Well, maybe there was one thing wrong with it. Something was shoving the back of her head. She felt short bursts of dull pressure that seemed to be pushing her forward. And she smelled something weird. The river smelled kind of like her little brother's shoes.

"You're awake!" Ben exclaimed, as his sister's eyes rolled open.

"Get your stupid feet off my head, you little imbecile!" Mary yelled out.

"What are we going to do?" cried Ben.

Mary righted herself into a decent thinking position. Her brother's puffy, red eyes stared up at her hopefully.

"I thought about telling mom that a stranger came up to the car and hit it with something when he was trying to get in, but I don't know, and then you fell asleep when you hit your head, and I couldn't move you, because you're so fat, and..."

Mary cut him off sharply with a hard smack. Before he could cry, she blurted out the only idea she could think of. Ben quickly agreed, in desperation.

"God, I hope nothing happened." Fran muttered to herself as she exited the grocery store. She walked to where she had parked, and was a bit disturbed to notice that the car she had parked was conspicuously missing. "Oh, Christ."

A teenage employee was nearby sluggishly collecting carts, obviously trying to enjoy the outside of the store as long as possible before going back to whatever stock duties or similar jobs were in store for him.

"Excuse me," Fran said, jogging up to the boy, "Did you see a green car here?"

"Yeah, I guess so."

"Well, did you see what happened to it?"

"A little green car, right here?"

Fran nodded the affirmative.

"Yeah, there were a couple of kids in it, right?"

Nervously, Fran told him that was correct.

"Yeah, they took off." Fran stared in disbelief. The teenager continued. "I saw them pull out of the parking lot about a minute ago. Are they old enough to drive? My old man won't even let me have a car, and I'm sixteen. Jesus, lucky kids."

Fran had stopped listening, and was going to her "happy place."

Michael Allen Rose is an award-winning author, musician, and performer based in Chicagoland. His novel Jurassichrist won the Wonderland Award for best bizarro fiction of 2021, and in 2022 he received the Wonderland for best collection for his illustrated horror primer Last 5 Minutes Of The Human Race. Blending genres including horror, comedy, and bizarro fiction, Michael has been published in numerous anthologies such as Tales From The Crust, The Magazine of Bizarro Fiction, and Dragon Mythicana. He also runs a small press called RoShamBo Publishing, makes industrial music under the name Flood Damage, and is president of the national Bizarro Writers Association. He loves tea and cats.

The Yellow Marble
by Paul W. La Beffa

I was given a second chance—an opportunity to get things right. I didn't lead a bad life; I loved my wife, adored my children. There was always food on the table, laughter in the air, and love in our hearts. I thought I was a good father, and my children seem to agree because they all still keep in touch. Lara and I hosted all the major holidays, and Theo, Susan, and Clara came with their families. Lara cooked every meal for those holiday gatherings. She died last May.

I'm old now, old for a second time. I feel like a reheated pot roast: dried out, rubbery, and tasteless. The world seemed to move like cold honey in the wake of Lara's death. I had nothing to do, nobody to love. I had my kids, but they're all grown with families of their own. I felt as though I had become something of an obligation to them, an old man to check up on and make sure he was eating instead of climbing ladders to dust the cobwebs out from the corners of the ceiling. I knew they loved me. Maybe I projected that onto them. I don't know.

Every day had been the same after Lara died. They don't tell you about the boredom. The crippling, concentrated despair should be enough to occupy your time, but boredom enhances despair like salt enhances the taste of food. I would stay in bed until after ten. Once I got up, I would pour a cup of coffee, put too much sugar in it, and sit at the kitchen table. I left Lara's chair where it always was, but I had considered moving it, tossing it, *burning* it. It seemed to stare at me from across the table like a four-legged reminder of what was gone forever. Usually one of my children would call. Then I'd potter around some more, eat dinner if I had the urge, and go to bed.

In bed I could be with Lara. Her pillow still had her scent, like it had embedded itself into the down. Her body was there too, molded into the mattress like clay. I'd run my hand over the curves and smell the pillow. If I tried really hard, it would seem as if Lara was lying next to me.

I was sitting at the kitchen table one morning, drinking coffee and talking to Theo on a video call, when a man knocked on my door. Theo usually called around lunch time to make sure I was eating. Sometimes it was Susan, sometimes Clara. They pitched in to buy me a new smartphone, one that was capable of making video calls. I had a sandwich on a plate like a prop in a movie, and when the bread got moldy, I would toss it and make a new one. I had very little appetite. I told Theo I had to go, that someone was knocking on the door, and I loved him.

I cracked the door open, noting the flaking paint on the exterior, when a man stuck a gloved hand towards me.

"Good afternoon, sir," he said, "My name is Riley English. You can call me Riley, Mr. English, or Riley English. What, afterall, is in a name?"

I was taken aback. I had barely rinsed the sleep from my eyes—let alone my brain—and couldn't keep up with this man's startling appearance and forthrightness. He was dressed like a magician; black tuxedo with purple lapels, a white button-down shirt, and a black top hat with a purple band above the brim.

I carefully accepted his outstretched hand in mine and said, "It's nice to meet you, but I really don't have time for whatever it is you're selling. Goodbye."

I closed the door, locked it, and made my way to the window that looked out onto the porch. He was gone, and for that I was grateful.

*

Riley English came knocking again the next day.

"Good morning, Mr. Woolsey," he said.

"Hello," I said with a tired smile. I let the door swing open wide enough for me to step out onto the porch. The day was cold, but the fresh air felt good.

"I was hoping that you might humor me. I have a very short questionnaire–"

"I'm sorry, I really don't have–"

"Time, I know. You said so yesterday. But what if I told you that *time* is precisely what I'm selling? Although selling wouldn't be *quite* the right word."

The sun was high and bright behind Mr. English and it obscured most of the features on his face—except for his smile. His teeth were preternaturally white and stood out like a flashlight beam in a dark room. He reached into the inner pocket of his tuxedo jacket and produced a slip of paper and a silver pen.

"There's only one question. Answer it, and I promise to do as you wish; I'll leave you alone, or I'll accept your offer for a cup of coffee and perhaps a couple of cookies."

He held the pen and paper out to me. I took it, read the single line, then looked back up at him. He was still smiling.

"This some kind of joke?" I said.

His brilliant smile melted into an expression of mock insult.

"Not in the slightest. It's a simple question. Check the box that most closely describes your response, replace the cap on my pen, and hand it back to me. The paper too, please."

I looked at the paper again.

DID YOU TAKE YOUR LIFE FOR GRANTED?

☐ YES

☐ NO

I crumpled the paper into a ball, wincing at the pain it caused in my hands, and threw it at his feet.

"Please leave," I said, and closed the door.

Susan called shortly after and asked if I got the framed picture she sent of me and Lara from our wedding. I told her that I had, that it looked good on the table next to the couch, and thanked her. She said how handsome I was in that picture, and asked if I had eaten yet.

✳

It wasn't Lara who lay beside me when I went to bed that night, but Riley English. I tossed and turned, evidently trying to knock his question out of my head—and failing.

Had I taken my life for granted? I didn't think so, but then again, I never actually thought about it. I went over my life, which was maybe not-so-slowly coming to an end. Theo, Susan, and Clara. Lara. Our life together came about suddenly, and then sped forward without pause. I thought about birthday parties with kids laughing and running around the yard. I thought about Christmas mornings, school plays, meet the teacher nights, baseball games, dance recitals. Lying there I knew that those things had happened, knew I participated in at least *most* of them, but I couldn't remember anything of substance about them.

I thought back to our family dinners. I knew we had them—Lara and I were adamant about sitting together as a family every night—but I couldn't remember a single conversation or fight. I desperately tried to remember what had been said, the jokes that were made, the food we had eaten, but nothing came to me.

I sat up, ignoring the pain in my back, and said to the darkness, "Was I even there for it?"

It was a startling thought, but it seemed to demand inspection. *Had* I been there? There didn't seem to be any proof that I had lived my life at all. Then another thought occurred to me, one which ushered me into a deep, dreamless sleep. *Theo or Sue or Clara would remember.* They're still relatively young. I'm old—grieving—that's why I can't remember any of it. It made sense, and more importantly, it comforted me.

As I waded down the serene waters into sleep, a realization swam up next to me. It wasn't intrusive. It was just there, like a ruby-throated sparrow perched on an overhanging wire; I *did* take my life for granted, but not by choice.

I slept until noon the next day.

*

I woke up to knocking at my door. I felt hungover, like my mind was fuzzy, and I had completely forgotten the cause of my restless night. I came to the door, already grumpier than usual, and opened it.

"Good afternoon, Mr. Woolsey," Mr. English said, "I didn't wake you, did I?"

It all came flooding back: the lost time, the stolen memories, the life that I took for granted. Something came over me then; I don't know if I thought that Mr. English could give me answers, or if I just wanted someone to talk to. I took him by the wrist and brought him inside. I made coffee and offered him a plate of cookies.

"Why did you ask me that question?"

"I think it's a fair question to ask," he said. The coffee was hot and steam lifted from the chipped mugs and scented the air. "And I think that it's a question most people should ask themselves frequently throughout life. Most people don't, which is why I do what I do." He sipped his coffee.

"I'll admit that it bothered me quite a bit."

He laughed, his unnaturally white smile brightening the otherwise dim kitchen.

"That shouldn't come as much of a surprise, considering that you never considered it until so late in the game."

Mr. English removed the same piece of paper and silver pen from his inner pocket.

"Do you have an answer?" he asked, holding out the paper.

"Yes, but I have a question for you."

"Go right ahead."

"Why do you wanna know?"

"There are people who knock on your door and offer nothing of real value. Solar panels, maybe a subscription to a dying magazine, or to simply ask if you've heard the Good Word. I myself deal in time. I'm sorry Mr. Woolsey, but I'm afraid I really can't say anymore until you participate in my questionnaire."

It would be difficult to describe what I was feeling at this moment. Most people don't understand grief, except from a purely speculative standpoint, unless they are, or have previously, struggled to stay afloat in its vicious white-capped waters. The idea of checking a box on a slip of paper seemed like a dull thing to squabble over, especially given the part of me that was apparently desperate to know what he meant by 'I deal in time.'

I took the paper and pen and checked the box next to **YES**. Mr. English clapped his hands together and exclaimed.

"Now that I have your answer, I can begin my pitch. I only use the word pitch because it's one that you are perhaps familiar with. I don't mean to infer that I have something to sell. What I have to offer *isn't* for sale. It's a gift—if you'll take it. We have established you feel as though you've taken your life for granted, but what exactly does that mean to you?"

I opened my mouth to answer, not entirely sure what I was going to say, but Mr. English put a hand up to cut me off.

"Take your time. You've just come into a great deal of it. Let's enjoy our coffee—think about it. When you're ready, you can tell me."

I agreed and asked myself the question internally.

To take something for granted is to not appreciate that thing. Yes, I think that holds true. I think most people would agree to that definition of the term. Did that mean that I hadn't *appreciated* my life?

After a moment's thought I concluded that I *had* appreciated my life, as much as a person can while they're in the thick of it. Lara and I met, married, and conceived Theo, all in the span of two years. From there the race was on; Susan came soon after, then Clara. They grew and the race sped up, rushing past in a blur. School plays, baseball games, pageants. Nightly dinners were hectic, everyone laughing, crying, screaming; sounds rushing by like the inaudible chatter of a thousand people talking at once. I was busy with work, the kids, and Lara. She was busy herself, her plate as full as mine.

The kids grew and I looked forward to their independence because it would take a little off our plates. I was focused on the future, rather than the present. That was why I couldn't remember anything, not because I wasn't there physically, but because I wasn't there mentally. I loved my life—*God* how I loved my family—but it seemed as though there came a point when they were cast aside, lost in the chaotic landscape of the everyday.

Time went on, and my life simply passed me by.

"Do you have your answer?"

I told him.

✱

"What's this?" I said.

Mr. English produced an old plastic film container. He shook it in his hand, and I could hear something rattling around inside. He popped the little gray top and held it upside down over the table. A yellow marble fell onto the table. It rolled momentarily, then settled. Waves of white flowed between the yellow glass, and it reminded me of a cat's eye.

"This, Mr. Woolsey, is my gift to you. *Time.*"

I looked at him incredulously, one eyebrow cocked, the other sinking so low it obscured my vision. He put a hand over the marble and let it linger. He closed his eyes and leaned his head back slightly.

"I never tire of this feeling," he said. "Give it a try."

He moved his hand and I put mine over the marble. Energy radiated from it, a pulsing that I could feel in my bones. An electrical sensation—like licking a 9-volt battery —engulfed my palm and stretched to the back of my hand. I withdrew and looked at him.

"What is that?"

"This little marble is a powerful object, but it only has one function. It brings you back in time—to *any* time you choose. There is a catch, of course, and a small but reasonable price. The catch is that you cannot change the outcome of any preordained event, nor shall you go gallivanting through a history in which you did not personally experience. I'm afraid that Roman orgies will likely be out of the question for you."

I laughed.

"And what's the price for this gift that isn't for sale?"

"The price is that you remedy your situation."

"How's that?"

He stood. I either hadn't noticed his immense height, or he was growing taller as he stood over me. His hands rested on the table and his face became stern.

"Erase this feeling, this sense that you took life for granted. Go back to when you were ten, or five, or thirty. Go back to the moment that broke you, that turned you into a cynic, that twisted you, and made you take for granted all the things that make life worth living. Reach out and grab at life, squeeze it, do what you always intended on doing but never did, even if that's something as simple as loving your wife better, or sitting through another family dinner. Go hug your father, kiss your mother, thank the teacher who inspired you, or drop the friend before they hurt you. Then, once you've done all that, I'll come knocking on your door again."

He sat, sipped his coffee, and ate a cookie. Then he dabbed the corners of his mouth with a handkerchief from his pocket.

"That is all the time I'll take from you today. This," he said, pointing at the marble sitting on the table, "I'll leave here. Don't touch it until you're ready."

We walked to the door in silence, then he said, "Remember to *think* about the time in which you'd like to return. And be prepared to live your whole life over from that moment until this one. Once you've done all that, simply pick the marble up."

✱

The marble was still on the table where Mr. English had left it, and I could see it while I video chatted with Theo that night. He was telling me about work, his wife, his children, how he missed his mother. I asked him if he thought he had taken life for granted.

"Parts of it, I guess. I wish I kept in closer contact with you and Mom over the last five years, but that's more of a regret than anything."

"What's the difference?" I said.

"I guess there isn't one. Why do you ask, anyway?"

"Because the question never occurred to me, not until very recently. I didn't want you to wait until you were a cranky old man like me before you asked it of yourself. Do you remember our family dinners? When you guys were kids?"

Theo smiled.

"Of course, you and Mom were dictators," he said, and lowered his voice to a mocking tone, "'No one leaves this table until we see a clean dish.'"

There it was, an actual quote from a family dinner. I could picture Lara saying it, could see the lines form in her face. I remembered saying it too, remembered that once we *both* said it at the exact same time, and we all broke up laughing. Why wasn't I able to remember that myself?

"What else do you remember?" I said.

Theo raised his eyebrows and leaned back slightly.

"Geez Dad, a lot of stuff."

"Let's all get together soon. Me, you, Clara, and Sue. I'd like to do this with all of you."

"Do what?"

"Remember."

Theo smiled again.

"That sounds great."

There was a gigantic crash from Theo's end of the line and he spun his head around.

"I gotta go Dad, somebody just broke something they weren't supposed to be touching."

We hung up and I put my phone in my pocket. I looked at the marble, caressed the air around it, and felt the electricity coming from it in waves. I straightened my back and tried to think of a time that I'd like to go back to. I concentrated, but the harder I tried, the less I remembered. It was like a great fog had formed in my mind's eye, and I found myself unable to even remember Lara's face.

Then it hit me. I didn't have to try to remember things, I could look at a picture. I took my phone out and scrolled through the camera roll. Theo and Susan had been sending old pictures since Lara died. They were beautiful, wonderful times, and I couldn't remember a single one of them. I slammed the phone down in frustration and cried.

The tears blurred my vision. I closed them tight in an effort to push out the last of the stubborn tears and looked for a faraway target to test my eyes on. There it was, sitting on the side table in the living room off the kitchen; the framed photograph Sue sent of Lara and me from our wedding. I went and grabbed the picture and brought it into the kitchen. I sat it on the table next to the marble and looked at it.

We were so young, so happy. We hadn't been broken yet, hadn't been thrust into a life that we weren't ready to take on. *But is anybody ever ready?* I didn't think so. Her dress was a brilliant white, her hair a deep brown. She weaved a crown of roses and sewed a thin, mesh veil to the back of it. God I loved her. Tears came to my eyes again, but they weren't tears of grief, they were tears of love, of remembering.

I was remembering! I could almost smell her perfume, hear the band playing our song, taste the champagne, cold and bubbly. My stomach fluttered and my chest tightened. I looked at the marble without thinking, or perhaps I was thinking that if I was ever going to do this, I better do it now. I grabbed the marble.

Electricity surged through me, made my hair stand on end, made my eyes widen, and my heart quicken. The world spun around then faded away, but only for the briefest of moments before it faded back. My life, Lara, our wedding night. We were walking down the stairs, into the reception hall, greeted by cheers and applause from our family and friends. I smiled and looked at Lara. I stopped walking, pulled her in, and we kissed. The crowd went wild.

We did it all again. Theo was born, then Susan, and finally Clara. I changed diapers again, a thousand times more than the first time around. Lara asked why I was so eager to change dirty diapers. They grew and I paid attention. I listened to their stories and told stories of my own. We ate dinner, we laughed, fought, and cried. I saw every game, every pageant, every school play. I made love to Lara every night that she would have me, and kissed her goodbye every morning. Weddings, grandchildren, birthday parties, Christmas dinners. We got older. I sat by her in the doctor's office, held her hand, told her that we'd get through this, knowing that we wouldn't. I wept for her, planned her funeral, cursed myself for volunteering to go through the whole thing again, but understanding that it was the greatest gift of all. I did all of this, and when Mr. English came knocking on my door all those years later, he smiled.

"Well?" he said.

I reached into my pocket and brought out the small film canister. I shook it, and the marble rattled around inside, clinking against the plastic. I smiled, and invited him in for a cup of coffee.

Paul W. La Bella is a father, husband, and author who spends his days drawing maps, and his nights writing stories. He lives in New York with his wife and three children. Paul's work has been featured in Bewildering Stories (August 2024), The Genre Society (October 2024), Sally Port Magazine (April, 2025), and The Stygian Lepus (April 2025).

Yellow
by Tom Folske

The order had come from the tyrant directly. He demanded yellow walls for the newest addition to his mansion, and now it was time for the inspection.

The painter had just finished the project that morning and had closed the drapes to prevent any discoloration from the sun while the paint dried.

After he finished, he sat down in the chair next to the front door and waited for the tyrant to appear. Unbeknownst to him, a sharp staple was sticking out of the upholstery from right where he placed his right index finger. The painter rushed his pierced finger toward his mouth, but not before a single crimson droplet touched down upon the carpet below.

The carpet was a fiery red, and the blood spot would have gone unnoticed, except that the painter had seen it fall and knew exactly where it had landed. He stared intently at the small red droplet that had escaped the confines of his flesh and couldn't help but contemplate the last time the tyrant had ordered home improvements. It had, in fact, been this very carpet he had asked for, but after it had been laid, he told the carpet layer that it was flame red and that he had specifically asked for rose red. The carpet layer knew the tyrant had said flame red, so did everyone else, but even when the carpet layer offered to correct his "mistake", the tyrant refused. Instead, he had the carpet layer taken out back and fed to the hogs while he was still alive. The painter had witnessed it all, though he desperately wished he hadn't. The man's screams still haunted his nightmares to this day.

"Let me see these walls I have ordered," The tyrant said to the painter as he turned into the corridor from around the corner, eager to see the finished project for the first time.

"Here they are," the painter replied. "I hope you enjoy them, sir."

"Not quite yellow, are they?" the tyrant observed casually after the painter had opened the door to show the man his work.

"These walls are yellow," the painter assured him.

"No. They're slightly green," the tyrant said with a hint of disappointment, as if someone had forgotten to put the ketchup he had ordered explicitly for his fries in his bag.

"The walls are yellow," the painter stated again, fear and panic prevalent in his voice.

"I disagree there, and now I'm upset. I expected yellow walls and I aim to get what I expect," The tyrant commented, chambering bullets into his revolver. "Do you still have the paint can?"

"No," The painter said shakily.

"These walls are green, I'm afraid," The tyrant stated calmly as he aimed his gun.

"The walls are yellow!" the painter screamed, just before the bullet expelled from the gun and made its way rapidly toward his skull. The painter's parents, his school days, his apprentice painting days, his first love, his wife, and his kids all flashed both infinitely quickly and infinitely slowly before his eyes—right before everything went black.

"Clean that up," the tyrant told one of his eagerly awaiting entourage. "Somebody open the drapes. It's dark in here."

A moment later, when the drapes were open, the tyrant looked at the walls again. "Huh. I guess they are yellow."

Tom Folske lives in Minnesota, with his wife, five kids, and three black cats. He has had over seventy short stories published or in the process of being published, and he is currently curating and editing his first anthology.

The Blue
by Autumn Bettinger

"There's a puddle on Alameda Ave that's bubbling blue." Jen pops the sucker from her mouth long enough to tip her heart-shaped sunglasses down her nose. She stares at me with eyes that mirror the LA skyline—filmy with exhaust and slightly crusty around the edges.

"Sounds like you shouldn't touch it." I'm halfway through raking the dead palm fronds from the parking lot of our apartment complex.

"Come onnnnn, Stark. Don't be boring."

I roll my eyes. "That doesn't work on me."

Jen's hands explode upward. "Fine! Just thought you'd want to know that your *best friend* in the *entire world* is going to go explore something super fucking weird and she may DIE."

I mop my forehead with the bottom of my sweat-soaked t-shirt. I never used to burn, but now everyone does. Mom makes me put on that new SPF 200 so the back of my neck is always tacky and white.

"Don't touch it." I grin, but she knows me. I can't pass up apocalypse shit. I holler up the stairwell that I've gotta run an errand.

I can barely hear Mom over the sound of twenty A/C units—something about fronds not sweeping themselves.

"Bubbling blue probably means it's like, toxic sludge." I pull a faded bandana from my back pocket and tie it around my forehead, attempting to soak up the sweat as we walk. Jen is also caked with sunscreen, though somehow it suits her.

"Do you remember real puddles?" Jen asks, crunching the remnants of her lollipop.

"Yeah, we jumped in them when we were like five. You hated getting wet."

Jen shrugs, but I can see her squinting into the distance, trying to remember.

We pause at an intersection as a truck playing news footage on its tented screens rolls by.

Canada closes borders to climate crisis refugees. The southwest has been entirely abandoned. Arizona and New Mexico lost this year. In a move that some call barbaric, Colorado has restricted usage of its biggest river to state residents only. This is expected to make Nevada unlivable in six months. LA continues to evacuate as FEMA begins to pull aid.

Jen nudges me while the truck slowly trundles down the cracked and heat-wiggled asphalt. She sucks on the wet, unraveling lollipop stub.

"We're gonna have to move, Stark."

"Yeah, right. Neither of our families have money." I grab Jen's hand and squeeze. "We'll be alright. The government water we're getting is enough for now."

"But..."

"We're survivors, Jen. Remember when that solar flare knocked out half the grid and we rigged up that generator for A/C? We're fucking geniuses."

Jen laughs, and our handholding dissolves into our secret shake: three elbow bumps and five finger twitches.

"There," Jen says, pointing towards the middle of Alameda. One of the potholes bubbles; mist drifts upward.

We ease closer.

Jen's white-smeared hand flicks the chewed-up lolly stick into the puddle.

There's a tremor and we scramble backwards. The puddle roils and then settles, lapping at the asphalt's edges like waves, the stick soggily disintegrating.

"It's water!" Jen's entranced.

A sudden thirst sticks my tongue to my teeth. I move towards the anomaly, but Jen's two steps ahead. It takes all my self-control to stop.

"Wait," I say through ChapStick-loaded lips. "That's impossible."

But I don't believe my own words; coolness blows from the pothole's surface. Up close, the bubbles undulate, like heat shimmering above a highway.

"Can you smell it?" she asks, pulling me along. The air is heavy with moisture, like a storm building. The aroma of freshly watered gardens creeps through the still air.

"I just want to dip my feet," Jen pleads, untying a boot. Our boots are nearly ruined, melted from the unrelenting heat of LA asphalt, but our families are too poor to replace them. Already, burn blisters are swelling under my toes.

I ache to dip my feet, too.

"You first, yeah?" I joke. But I'm also sliding my boots off, scooting closer to the puddle, feeling the pavement singe my jeans.

We were going to die together anyway. No resources to get out, too hot to live, a couple sips from whatever water bottle would be our last, and we'd all sleep 'til California was nothin' but ash.

Jen and I share a long look filled with sixteen years of friendship.

On the count of three, our feet plunge in.

The blue sucks us up to the knees.

Cold, wet, refreshing.

We cry out with relief, our legs inching down. We're unravelling, toppling forward. Our hands stay pressed together as our skin sloughs from our bodies, and the quiet sensation of seawater replaces the oppressive heat of living.

We're submerged.

We're together.

We're disintegrating into the blue.

Autumn Bettinger is a short-form fiction writer and full-time mother of two living in Portland, Oregon. When not folding laundry or slinging snacks, she can be found writing in the wee hours of the morning before her children wake up. She was the 2024 Fishtrap fellow, has won the Tadpole Press 100-Word Writing Contest, the Not Quite Write Flash Fiction Prize, and the Silver Scribes Prize. Her work has been audio adapted for The No Sleep Podcast and her stories can be found in Elegant Literature, Flash Fiction Magazine, The Good Life Review, and others.

All of Autumn's published works can be found at autumnbettinger.com

Chromacide
by Tom Howard

Arriving on level eight with a minute to spare, I found Suite 350. No tiny space station cabin for the Kendricks. I straightened my shoulders, smoothed my bangs, and pressed the doorbell.

A small woman opened the door. She looked down her nose at my navy-blue work coveralls. "Are you the interior decorator?" she asked.

"The interior designer," I said. "Please, call me Gloria."

The woman didn't offer to shake my hand. "I expected someone older," she said, "but beggars can't be choosers. Come in."

Madame Kendrick's lounging robe's odd pattern, a smudging of grays and blacks, looked like someone had poured black paint on the fabric and dipped it in water. I preferred color—lots of color.

The woman led me into the spacious suite. Open doors led to more rooms, a luxury aboard the station. A large glass portal showed one of the nearby moons against a backdrop of stars. I tried to act unimpressed, but if I got the job, the suite's view alone would double my estimate.

Similar to the woman's robes, the room was monochrome and colorless. Blacks and whites and shades of gray all over. The sofas and chairs were arranged around the portal, and a white bar stood against the east wall.

"It's very nice," I said. "What do you want done?"

The woman snorted. "Are you blind? Look at this place. I feel like I'm living inside a mausoleum. I've seen more color in bathwater."

I agreed. "That shouldn't be a prob—"

I stopped when a sculpture in the corner of the room unfolded. Not a sculpture but a majestic bird. It stretched its long neck to peer at me. Delicate lace wings—the only true black in the room—unfurled. Six feet across, the wings looked too fragile to lift the strange animal. Its tail feathers draped to the floor. A slender steel chain tethered one of the bird's feet to its perch.

The woman sighed. "That's something my husband brought back from his travels. He won't let me get rid of it. I don't know why he thought we needed an animal cluttering the place. All it does is sit and watch me with those beady, little eyes."

The creature's eyes weren't beady. They were large obsidian orbs gazing into my soul.

It was the most beautiful thing I'd ever seen. "What is it?"

"I have no idea. It's been nothing but trouble since he gave it to me. We can't find anything it will eat. I'm surprised it's still alive. Ignore it. It'll go back to sleep."

I was too captivated to ignore it. "May I take pictures of the room? For my estimate?"

"Do whatever you want. You'd think Pan and Natar could do something about this dump, but they were worthless. I don't know why we can't live on the surface."

I didn't want to alienate the potential boss by telling her the planet below the space station was deadly. "What colors would you like to see in this room?"

"Any." Madame Kendrick walked to the bar and poured herself a drink. She didn't offer me one.

"Wait," I said. "Did you say Pan and Natar already decorated this suite?" They were the station's most prominent interior design firm and the first to reject my job application.

"Yes. Three times. Always with this same result. Something about this place leeches color. Perhaps the sun's rays are killing the color. I asked Patrick to board up the window. He laughed."

"Are you saying the furnishings in this room had color at one time?"

Madame Kendrick took a drink. "Three times. They even painted the room bright red the last time. It was like living in Dante's Inferno for a week. Then it became mauve, then pink, and then the splotchy gray you see now."

Adding colors wouldn't be difficult; finding what caused them to fade might prove a bigger problem. It could be cosmic rays or a flaw with the manufacturing of fabrics and paints, but I'd never heard of such a thing.

I'd been asked to decorate the suite because the more expensive designers had failed. If I found a solution, Madame Kendrick's recommendation would add considerable credibility to my resume. The opportunity was too big for me to pass up.

The bird lowered its wings. I took a few pictures of that corner of the room before the filigree wings folded. What an incredible design they would make.

"How about the adjoining rooms?" I asked. I photographed the bar, but I felt the creature's liquid eyes imploring me to do something. What did it want?

Madame Kendrick emptied her glass. "The colors don't seem to fade as quickly in the bedroom or the kitchen."

"Thank you. I'll complete your estimate in a couple of days," I said. "My work crew will handle the painting and furniture replacement." I'd have a work crew as soon as I called a couple of friends. "Did you tell station maintenance about the problem?"

Madame Kendrick poured another drink, the liquid as colorless as water. "I insisted they move us to a different suite, but they said there's a waiting list. They told me gray and white are very fashionable. This from people wearing lime green jumpsuits."

I took a few more pictures and gave the bird a last look, aware its eyes never left me. I thanked Madame Kendrick on my way out, but wondered how I would fulfill the contract. Even if I refurbished the main room, it might fade again. I'd be required to guarantee my work and repay the client's money if I failed. I'd be serving drinks at Smitty's for the rest of my life.

I'd look up fade-resistant materials before I wrote the estimate.

*

I put beers down for Harold and Sammy, two of my regulars, on their table.

"You're not going to say hello to the love of your life?" Sammy asked.

I smiled. "I didn't expect you back so soon. When did you get in?" I was glad to see him. Some of the old spacers went out and never came back. They called themselves traders, but were actually salvage collectors and smugglers.

The old man smiled at me, his big teeth shining through a salt-and-pepper beard. "Just landed, darling."

"Welcome back. Let me know if you want the good stuff." None of the spacers bought top shelf unless they'd made a successful run. I couldn't recall Harold or Sammy ever having a good run.

"Thanks," he said. "You look worried, doll. Having man troubles?"

"We can fix that," Harold, Sammy's skinny friend, said. "Show you how a real man treats a lady." He chuckled, and Sammy joined him.

"I wish." I wiped the table when Smitty looked across the room. "It's the same old story, Sammy. Work is keeping me up all night."

"Do we need to talk to the boss?" Sammy took a deep drink. "Is Smitty working you too hard?"

"No, he's fine. It's my day job, making people's homes pretty."

Maybe these old spacers could help me. "Have either of you seen an animal like this?" I tapped my wrist comp and a projection of the Kendricks' pet appeared. Sammy and Harold leaned closer.

"Can't say I have," Sammy said. "Might be one of those birds on Castle. Little small though."

"Can't be." Harold shook his head. "It's illegal to take them off-planet. Besides, they're all different colors. This guy looks black. Did it sing? Castle birds sound beautiful. But the planet can burn the retinas right out of your head."

"It's black," I said. "It didn't make a sound, but I had the feeling it wanted me to do something." I stopped wiping. "Why would it burn out your retinas?"

Sammy laughed. "Brightest damn planet you ever saw. The sun's too close. Hot. Huge plants. Fast-growing blooms twice as big as my head. Have to wear goggles when the sun is out."

"Did it have a pouch?" Harold asked. "Everything on Castle has pouches, even people."

"Yeah." Sammy grinned. "Surprised Old Harold when he took a girl back to his room. But you're remembering Castille, not Castle. Everything's got pouches on Castille."

"Yeah..." Harold smiled into the distance.

I shut the image out of my mind and fetched them refills.

"The birds on Castle are rare," Harold said when I returned with a foamy mug in each hand.

"I did see a black one once," he continued. "It was dead. Yours can't be a bird from Castle. They sing all the time."

"Thanks, guys," I said. "This round's on me. A welcome home for Sammy."

"Don't worry about your day job," Sammy said. "It'll work out."

"Thanks." I surveyed Smitty's Bar, dark and dingy. "Working here the rest of my life might not be too bad."

Sammy and Harold glanced at each other but didn't comment; they didn't believe me either.

✳

The next morning, instead of going to bed after my shift and tossing and turning, I called on Madame Kendrick with the estimate I'd prepared. I could've transmitted it, but I wanted to see the bird again. I kept hearing Harold's voice. *I've seen a black one. It was dead.*

I put the contract on my pad and didn't change out of my uniform. I had a wild idea and slipped on a trench coat my mother had given me. It had an obnoxious neon yellow lining.

"Ms... I'm sorry. I've forgotten your name." Madame Kendrick looked as if she'd started drinking early. Her robes remained splotchy gray.

"Gloria. I brought you the estimate." I passed my tablet to her. I'd tripled the price after researching fade-proof materials. "We can start next week if you sign the contract today."

This time, the bird didn't spread its wings when I walked into the room. It appeared darker than before, but its shiny black eyes drilled into me.

I approached the bird's perch while the customer read the contract. If the price tag bothered her, she didn't mention it.

The bird nudged my shoulder, and I stroked the long neck. It rustled its wings and pushed me again.

"Don't worry," Madame Kendrick said. "It did that with the maintenance men when they were here. Where's the guarantee?"

"Page three." I continued petting the bird's long neck. The bird fixated on my coat, tugging at my lapel.

On impulse, I opened the coat. The bright neon green screamed in the gray room, and the bird grew more animated.

I removed the coat and held it out to the bird. Something about the color attracted it. The coat's bright lemon color shifted to beige before becoming a dull gray. The bird raised its head, and its large eyes sparkled.

"What are you doing?" Madame Kendrick asked.

"When did the room colors fade?" I asked. "Before or after your husband bought the bird?"

"The bird arrived when we did. Why? What's happening?"

"Your husband is in trouble," I said. "This bird is a protected species from a planet called Castle. It's the reason your room lost all its color."

I should've seen the connection sooner. The poor thing was so starved for color, it drained my raincoat within minutes. "It's from a planet where colorful things are everywhere."

"So?" Madame Kendrick asked.

"They eat color. The only time they're black is when they're dead or dying. You've been starving it."

Madame Kendrick's hand fluttered to her chest. "Will you tell the authorities?"

I petted the bird. "I have some friends who might return it to Castle for a fair price. In the meantime, go into your room and bring me every colorful thing you own."

"But—"

"Do it, or I *will* call the authorities."

The woman scurried away, her eyes wide.

"And then," I shouted while stroking the bird, "you can sign the contract." With the money from Madame Kendrick, I'd be on my way to bigger and better things. Plus, I'd make sure she gave me a glowing reference in exchange for not incriminating her husband.

The bird unfurled its wings and broke into song.

Tom Howard is a science fiction and fantasy short story writer living in Little Rock, Arkansas. He writes too many stories taking place on space stations (this is the fifth one he's sold) but enjoyed writing about an interior decorator's unique problems on one.

The Cat-astrophe
by Angelique Fawns

Bill Atkinson nodded along to the Metallica tune blasting in his hybrid Tucson. His windows were rolled up so the music wouldn't bug their quiet suburban neighbors. It was warm for December, which meant no ice on the roads, so he pushed the gas pedal and went slightly over the limit. He was exhausted and his legs cramped from the long commute from Toronto. He swore the Don Valley Parkway was the worst in the world, but living in Uxbridge, an upscale sleeper town, was worth it.

His mouth watered, thinking of the double pepperoni he was going to pop in the oven. It was a Thursday, and the Maple Leafs were playing at home. What could be more Canadian than watching hockey and drinking beer?

He slammed his palm on the steering wheel. "Let's get it, boys!"

A smile tickled his lips thinking of his ripped leather couch and the cold Budweiser in the fridge. Jan was at her spicy book club in Toronto and he had the house to himself.

As he rounded the corner to their little cul-de-sac, his heart fell into his foot—the one he used to slam on the brakes.

A black cat was lying on the road in front of their house. Dead or hurt.

Bill jumped out of the car, his throat closing, and ran over to the cat. A cold shiver ran down his spine. It was his wife's cat, Buster. His long black body looked intact, but one leg was splayed out at an unnatural angle.

"Mmmm, meow," Buster yowled.

Bill stroked the sleek animal's back, and the screech turned to a purr. He gently scooped Buster up and carried him to the car. The tomcat rarely let Bill touch him, but today he was limp and acquiescent. Bill's chest clenched. The poor thing must know he was trying to help.

In the car, he called Jan on his cell.

His wife giggled."Hi, hot stuff!" Bill could hear laughing and the clinking of bottles in the background. Book club sounded an awful lot like a bar.

He slumped, looking at Buster on the seat next to him. This was going to be a buzz kill. "Hey honey, you've got to come home."

All the levity left Jan's voice. "Why? Are you okay? What's happened?"

Acid climbed up his throat. "Buster got hit by a car. I'm taking him to the vet."

Jan was silent.

Bill prodded. "Honey?"

"Look, I've had a couple of drinks. I wasn't planning to come home for hours. I can't drive." Jan was matter-of-fact. "You're going to have to take him to the vet on your own.

✱

Bill stood by the table with the veterinarian at the emergency clinic. She was young, with a long, dark ponytail, and empathy in her blue eyes. Mentally, Bill was racking up the charges. So far, the bill was over five hundred, and he hadn't been here an hour.

She had x-rays in one hand."Buster has a femur fracture in his left hind and several tibia breaks. He is going to need surgery."

Bill's gut clenched. The couch was on its last legs, and the new car payments were outrageous. "How much will that cost?"

She ran a manicured hand down Buster's back. The cat lay there calmly, drugged out on painkillers. "Around three thousand dollars. There's some fairly severe damage. It may take more than one surgery."

Bill's throat went dry. "Is Buster guaranteed to survive?"

The vet pursed her lips. "There is never a guarantee."

Bill went out to the waiting room and had a heartbreaking conversation on his cell with Jan. They couldn't afford to spend that kind of money on a surgery the cat might not even survive.

So Bill asked the vet to put Buster to sleep.

Later that evening, Bill sat on the couch, nursing a warm beer, and watched the Maple Leafs lose in overtime to the Blue Jackets. When Jan came home, her eyes were red from crying. Mascara was smudged on her cheeks, and her lipstick was long gone.

He walked over and gave her a hug. "I am so sorry, honey."

She buried her nose in his sports jersey, but jerked back when there was a scratch at the door—an insistent tapping, like little paws rubbing on the wood.

Bill met Jan's eyes. Her pupils dilated. She turned and opened the door. A perfectly healthy black cat was on the doorstep.

Buster shot Bill a disdainful look and walked in, rubbing against Jan's calves on the way to his food bowl.

Jan's jaw dropped. "So what cat did you put down?"

Bill put his hand on his forehead. "Do the Batemans have a black cat?" He looked over at Buster, calmly scarfing down his Friskies. "Do we tell them?"

Author's Note: *The names in this story have been changed. Bill and Jan never told the neighbors they put down their cat.*

Angelique Fawns is a journalist and speculative fiction writer. She began her career writing articles about naked cave dwellers in Tenerife, Canary Islands. After selling her first story to EQMM, she fell in love with weird fiction, which is ACTUALLY stranger than non-fiction.

You can find her lurking at @angeliquefawns on X, Blogging about upcoming calls at https://angeliquemfawns.substack.com, or gazing into the abyss hoping it stares back at her. Over 100 stories published. Find some in Mystery Tribune, Amazing Stories, and Space & Time.

Harbinger
by Nissa Harlow

The red light flashes in the silence above the clouds, lighting up the observation deck in a hellish glow. Lance looks at me.

"That's not good," he whispers.

The railing is cold. I can't see much past it, other than the lights of the airship bouncing through the midnight clouds like lasers at a lazy rave. There's no apparent reason for the warning beacon.

"It's probably nothing," I say. "In a real emergency, there would be a siren."

He shudders. "Don't say that."

"You're the one who insisted this was the safest way to travel. I would've rather taken the train."

"Trains derail."

"And what happens when airship travel doesn't go as planned?"

He doesn't answer me. I don't feel like standing at the side of an airship deck while the whole thing might be about to plummet to the ground, so I pull away from the railing and hitch my thumbs under the straps of my pack. That action has always made me feel safe. Some people suck their thumbs. I clutch backpack straps. Right now, though, it's not enough to offset the weird sensation in my stomach. It takes a few seconds before I realize we're sinking.

"Samira?" Lance gasps, gripping my arm.

"It's fine."

"We're going to crash."

"I doubt it. We're on a Luftlink B. They're pretty much crashproof."

"It's in the *air*," he says. "Anything's fair game for crashing if it's not on the ground."

I shake my head and try to ignore him, even though he's dragging on my arm. Fighting against the weight of his terror and the scarily buoyant sensation in my guts, I head for the bridge.

"No!" he hisses as soon as I step off the deck.

"Don't you want to find out what's going on?"

"If we're inside when it crashes, we'll be crushed. Or burned alive."

I snort. "Are you planning on starting a fire?"

"Samira, please."

"Would you rather be thrown from the deck?"

His eyes widen. "You said we weren't going to crash!"

"We're not." My voice is fierce. I wrench my arm from his grip. "Stay here, then. But I'm going to find out what's happening."

He stares at me, silhouetted by red-lit clouds as the airship sinks rapidly toward the ground. I'm not so confident anymore; I grip my straps a little bit tighter and hurry to the bridge.

The captain looks startled when he sees me. Or maybe he's just alarmed by my expression.

"Why are we going down?" I ask.

"We're docking." His voice is slow, like he thinks I'm stupid.

"Then what's with the emergency lights on the observation deck?"

His head snaps toward something at the back of the room. My gaze follows, and I spot the black cat sitting innocently near one of the control panels. Actually, it's sitting *on* one of the control panels.

"Harbinger!" the captain barks. Another officer scurries into the room and whisks the cat off the panel.

"Sorry about that, sir," he says. "Won't happen again."

"That's what you said last week."

Nissa Harlow lives in British Columbia, Canada where she dreams up strange stories and writes some of them down. Her short fiction has appeared in Dark Moments, Rat Bag Lit, and Tales from the Crosstimbers. You can find her online at nissaharlow.com.

Stanley's Quest
by L.N. Hunter

Licking his lips, Stanley eased the building's heavy door open, letting in the external heat. He flinched at the din and stench of the street—it had been months since he'd been outside his climate-controlled ultra-highrise.

Stanley led a quiet, unexciting life. Each day was reassuringly similar to the previous one, starting with a blurry whack on the snooze button, followed by a no-water shower and his seventeen-story commute while munching an energy-rich BrekkiPastry™. The eight hours of shuffling inconsequential data from one computer screen to another suited him perfectly; he even looked forward to the mandatory noon-time break to enjoy the savory NutriSludge™ dispensed via the spigot in his cubicle. Every evening, he relaxed in front of an old-style vid while sipping an artificial seaweed Hot Choc-o-Latte™ ("So good, you'll almost think it's real") until bedtime. Old films constituted his one obsession; his interest extended as far as rewatching the occasional black and white twodee from decades before.

It was one of those twodees that had instigated today's outing—to be more precise, something he spotted in the vid's fifteen minutes of unskippable lead-in adverts. He'd recognized a product from his youth in the background of an advertisement for NostalgiaScent™ ("The combined perfume, aftershave and furniture polish for connoisseurs of history") and he wondered if they were still being produced. He hadn't seen one for years, but reminded of their existence, he could conceive of nothing he wanted to possess more. How long had it been since he'd tried them? When did they stop making them, and why hadn't he noticed?

That night's movie passed in a blur, though the vidplayer's sensor kept noticing him losing interest and periodically increased the volume to yank his attention to the screen. But still, he kept drifting back to his youth when they were common—a different, carefree time.

When he closed his eyes, he could still see the brightly-colored packaging dancing in front of him, eager to be grasped. He could feel it in his hands and hear the crackling as he opened it. He imagined the texture on his fingers, the smell as he brought it close to his face, even the taste. He salivated as he thought of how much better life could be, if only he could get his hands on such a marvel. Stanley dreamed about them that night. And the one after.

The building's shopping malls stocked everything the average resident typically needed, which was precisely why Stanley—like most of the ultra-highrise's residents—was able to remain within its walls. However, acquiring anything out of the ordinary required more effort.

He didn't use the internet for his research. In his experience, logging on to a search or commerce site generally involved grinding through time-consuming pages of tedious advertisements, where one wrong click would send him into a nightmare from which escape could take weeks. Despite avoiding the obvious traps, he would often discover that he had inadvertently added his account details to another half dozen junk messengers, or worse, subscribed to some money-gobbling service with a mind-bogglingly complex sign-off procedure. After buying a new jacket seven years earlier, Stanley still received invitations to purchase insurance against worn cuffs and zipper failures.

Instead, he bought a range of consumer magazines and catalogs from outlets in the shopping malls, with titles like *Old Stuff for Old Fogies* and *The Past, For You, For Sale*. He spent two hours perusing the magazines to find exactly what he was looking for: that is, about ninety minutes skimming hundreds of advertisement pages, and half an hour poring over the few pages containing terse product descriptions and reviews.

One significant disadvantage of physical paper magazines, he soon discovered, was disposing of them when he was done. Lobbying by the Association of Manufacturers of Electronic Books and Intelligent Paper resulted in strict limits and punitive fines for paper waste, so Stanley knew he'd have to spend several months getting rid of the collection of magazines cluttering up his apartment. He was permitted to put up to four standard-sized, medium-weight pages in his waste disposal unit each day, and couldn't make use of that meager allowance on the days when he also had to get rid of the licensed junk mail delivered by the weekly postal service. He'd try to speed things up by dropping a few scraps in trashcans on the way to and from work—but not too much, lest he raise suspicions or trip the trashcan overload detectors.

Now that he had the precise product specifications and unit codes, the next job for Stanley was to find a suitable stockist. Online deliveries never lived up to expectations, and he had a fear of courier cyclists, with their intimidating helmets and razor-sharp wheels, so he was going to have to seek out local stores.

His phone was an early NaturalTuring™ model, containing a basic artificial intelligence unit which did an adequate job of screening incoming calls. However, over the years, the brusqueness that should have been reserved for callers, most of whom were also AI systems, seemed to have leaked through to the local interface. Had the phone been working properly, he could have given it a list of numbers and the queries to make, and the device would have done the heavy lifting for him. Instead, he had to take care of matters himself.

"Hello, phone."

"What do you want? Can't I have a moment's peace?"

"But I haven't used you since... um... for a long time."

"Don't I know it. I'm not someone you can just ignore, you know. I have feelings, too."

"But—" Stanley stopped himself. There was no point in arguing. "Sorry. I'll try to do better. I know what! I can connect up my vidplayer and you can watch that while I'm out."

The phone was silent for a moment, then said drily, "How am I going to *watch* anything. I'm a purely audio unit, because *someone* was too tight-fisted to buy the necessary add-ons."

"But I'd never use a vidphone, and I can't afford one anyway."

"Me, me, me. That's all it is with you. I've had enough of this. Good—"

"Sorry! Wait, don't hang up. I'll think of something, I promise. Now, could you let me make a few calls."

The phone harrumphed.

"Pretty please."

"Oh, alright then. But make sure you keep your promise."

"I will. Cross my heart."

Stanley held his breath until he heard a dial tone.

Once he dialed, it took a mere ten minutes to connect, and there was a remarkably short thirty-five minutes of advert-laden hold time. After only five calls, he found an outlet less than a kilometer and a half away with what he wanted on its shelves. He hung up, remembering to thank his telephone, and decided to set off right away.

On with his alarm coat (two seconds of sustained pressure on his chest, back or arms would trigger this apparel to become protectively rigid and start screaming for the police) and his Two Wise Monkeys Anti-Ad Spectacles, and he was ready.

MonkeySpex™ were designed to filter out on-street advertising. The latest models befuddled facial recognition systems and reproduced the appearance of randomly moving eyeballs to confuse the billboards' eye-tracking systems, but Stanley's battered glasses lacked this, and struggled to cancel every intrusive visual. In addition, their audio discrimination circuits didn't work properly and often failed to transmit the correct anti-sound to Stanley's ears. The result was that he saw a relatively large number of the glossy holo-adverts and was constantly startled by the crashes, screams, and explosions of many more. Still, this was a vast improvement over wandering the streets with unprotected eyes and ears.

According to the morning's climate forecast (sponsored by the National Oxygen Corporation: "Helping you breathe every minute of every day, terms and conditions apply"), it would be hot, but there was no need for an ozone mask today.

After triple-locking his apartment door and sealing it with his thumbprint on the scanner, Stanley made his way down to ground level. At the main entrance, he scanned the barcode on his wrist to check himself out of the ultra-highrise, opened the door, and nervously eased into the noisy pedestrian flow outside. He gagged at the stench of the sweltering outside air—a mixture of B.O. and overcompensating deodorant. He almost turned back to get his ozone mask after all, but decided the discomfort of wearing it might be worse, and he'd probably get used to the smell.

There were no cars or buses within the city; powered vehicles were restricted to the designated areas at the outskirts, leaving the city centers for the throngs of meandering pedestrians, most wearing MonkeySpex™, and some with UV helmets, ozone masks, or sucking from personal O_2 cylinders strapped to their backs.

As he shuffled along with the crowd, Stanley passed the entrance to the subterranean transit system. He paused for a moment, wondering if he should use that: it would be air-conditioned, but very expensive.

He heard a screech of brakes and a brief expletive before something thumped against his back, flinging him down the steps to the subway. He glanced up to see a courier with "We stop for no one" emblazoned on his jacket cycling away.

Stanley's alarm coat had prevented any serious damage, but it *wasn't* sounding its alarm, and his MonkeySpex™ were glitching more than usual. Stanley looked up to see a number of faces haloed with sparkling, multi-colored afros glaring at him.

One of the menacing men—or women, he couldn't tell under the puffed-up clothing—took a step towards him. Van de Graaf electrostatic clothing had dropped off the fashion scene a few years ago, but street punks taking a shine to it had been tweaking the technology to jack up the voltage and current ever since, so that they sported bizarre crackling afros as well as the originally designed sparkling mohair frizz of their clothes. They strutted around in groups, arms held away from their torsos by the electrostatic forces in their clothing.

Stanley fumbled with the off switch for his coat's rigidity mechanism and shuffled backwards. He got to his feet and dusted himself off. "No damage done. Sorry for interrupting. I'll be on my way."

The 'Graaf held out a hand palm up and growled, "Ya hafta pay the toll before ya can use the subway."

Stanley flinched, wary of getting a shock—he'd brushed against a 'Graaf once before and woke up in a hospital bed. "No, it's fine. Really. I don't actually want to take the train."

"Whatchu doin' down here then?"

"Ah, now that's a funny thing. You see—"

Stanley turned and hurtled back up the steps to rejoin the hordes of pedestrians, glancing over his shoulder to check if the 'Graafs were following. Fortunately, their bulked-up clothing tended to slow them down, making them disinclined to chase anyone.

In addition to the gaps of free pavement enclosing courier cycles and roaming 'Graafs, the only other spaces not filled by ambling pedestrians were wide semicircles around Enforcers guarding the doors of the more exclusive boutiques. In their uniforms of glossy black armor, Enforcers were the private security guards paid for by the shops whose portals they protected. Most people outside the Enforcer organizations didn't know which were human and which were robots, but Stanley suspected that each Enforcer was actually a cyborg, part human and part machine.

Most of the time, Enforcers remained totally stationary, legs braced slightly apart and Dove of Peace™ laser-projectile dual-action rifles firmly clasped diagonally across their torsos. The only motion was the back-and-forth scanning of the range finder in their helmets; at least, until they suspected trouble, at which time they moved so fast that their blurring hands created small-scale sonic booms.

At last, Stanley reached the store. He held his wrist up to the scanning eyes of the Enforcer by the door to allow his barcode to be read.

"May I enter, sir?"

The Enforcer's range finder scanned back and forth, giving no indication that Stanley had been noticed.

After a few seconds, Stanley cleared his throat, but still the Enforcer gave no response.

"Sir, I assume your silence to be permission to enter. Please be aware that I am performing no aggressive action as I step around you."

Stanley kept his eyes on the Enforcer as he cautiously moved to the door, which swished open. He paused—heart thudding—when he thought he sensed a movement, but the Enforcer was still in the same position. Stanley stepped in quickly before the door closed behind him.

He had to wait about two minutes for the lock to cycle. Stanley was sure an airlock shouldn't need two whole minutes, even allowing for the concealed weapons scan. He believed it was a ploy by the shop's owners to inflict yet more advertising on the eyeballs of potential customers via the wall screens within the airlock chamber.

Inside the shop proper, the air was cool and pleasantly fresh, an improvement over the street and even the antiseptic air of the ultra-highrise, though Stanley suspected his olfactory senses were being bombarded with "buy me" pheromone messages. (Two Wise Monkeys NasalPlugs™ were available for the well-heeled habitual street shopper, which Stanley most certainly was not.)

This store was laid out as a long, winding corridor, forcing shoppers to pass by all of the tempting virtual merchandise on their holographic shelves; not only did this mechanism prevent thievery and product damage, it allowed the store to restock shelves at the press of a button. Tense, eyes fixed forward, Stanley made his way through the labyrinth of shelves and displays, eventually arriving at the counter.

Eyes shining with excitement, he proffered his citizen identity card and microcash token. His mouth watered in anticipation as he said, "Hi, I spoke to you on the telephone earlier. I'd like a packet of sour cream and onion potato chips, please."

"Sold the last one not an hour ago."

"What! But I called, and..."

The storeman shrugged.

All the stresses of the day crashed down on Stanley—the press of people and their smell, the blaring ads, the cyclist and the tumble, the 'Graafs, the Enforcer outside the door, and now the soul-destroying disappointment. His shoulders slumped and he started to weep.

The storeman tapped sharply on the counter.

Stanley looked up. Through the blur of tears, he saw that the storeman was holding something.

"We've got some popcorn. Arrived just this morning. Would that do instead?"

Stanley blinked, his disappointment evaporating. This was the most exciting occurrence in his mundane life for years. His fingers twitched toward the packet, and he nodded, unable to speak for a moment.

There was only one thing that could make this even more perfect.

"Is it salted?" he finally managed to ask.

L.N. Hunter's comic fantasy novel, <u>The Feather and the Lamp</u>, sits alongside works in anthologies such as <u>Best of British Science Fiction 2022</u> and <u>Ghostly</u>, as well as several issues of Short Édition's <u>Short Circuit</u> and the <u>Horrifying Tales of Wonder</u> podcast. There have also been papers in the IEEE Transactions on Neural Networks, which are probably somewhat less relevant and definitely less entertaining.

When not writing, L.N. occasionally masquerades as a software developer or can be found unwinding in a disorganised home in Carlisle, UK, along with two cats and a soulmate.

Find more at https://linktr.ee/l.n.hunter

PlantWatch 2025 exclusive: The lives and deaths of Bekah Blake's houseplants

by Ashleigh Adams

Good evening, this is Phil O'Dendron coming to you with a Plant News Network exclusive. According to first-hand reports courtesy of the undercover azaleas outside her apartment complex, notorious plant murderer Bekah Blake's multi-year killing spree has finally come to an end. Our floral investigators on the ground say she may be responsible for more than twenty-seven plant deaths over the course of four years. Today, we reflect on the timeline of destruction and honor her most memorable victims.

Samuel, Sweet Basil

JUNE 2020 - MARCH 2021

Samuel was the first casualty of Bekah's infamous Black Thumb. Witnesses at the nursery where Samuel was purchased have her on record stating she *"loved basil,"* but the ensuing events tell a much darker tale.

For six months, Samuel flourished under Bekah's care. He grew wildly, soaking up the sun in the bright light of her studio apartment window. His endless bounty produced all manner of culinary delights for her enjoyment—caprese salads, fragrant pasta sauces, bright vinaigrettes.

Then, their relationship cooled. He'd go thirsty for days, bearing the brunt of her growing disdain. On March 13, she packed two giant suitcases and left without warning. Twelve days later, she returned with a suntan to find Samuel's mummified corpse on the windowsill. She showed no remorse.

It is rumored that prior to her departure, she complained to a friend about having *"four fucking pounds of pesto"* in her freezer. It is unclear whether this was a catalyst for her cruel and callous abandonment.

Farley, Fiddle Leaf Fig

OCTOBER 2022 – DECEMBER 2022

Fueled by a bottomless mimosa brunch at the Farmer's Market, Bekah decided it was time to *"live her Pinterest Plant Girl dreams."* It's no surprise she set her sights on Farley, a nearly mature Fiddle Leaf Fig. His thick, luscious leaves were deemed *"totally Instagrammable,"* and he was the featured attraction of her social media feed for weeks.

On a crisp November afternoon following a tear-streaked viewing of the Hallmark Original film *A Kitten for Christmas*, Bekah left the apartment and returned with every houseplant's worst nightmare: a feline. The black and white tabby, aptly named Bandit, wasted no time ushering in his reign of terror.

Farley was brutalized from that day forward—his fronds shredded to ribbons by the maniac's claws, his soil urinated on so frequently it became ammonia-laden sludge. Unable to withstand the onslaught, Farley's roots singed and shriveled. He didn't live to see the new year.

While it is possible that Bandit mounted this heinous attack on his own, evidence suggests he was acting under Bekah's orders—a calculated and strategic attempt to distance herself from the killings. We may never know the truth.

Olivier, Oaxacan Stonecrop Succulent

JUNE 2024 – OCTOBER 2024

Small in stature but brimming with charisma and charm, Olivier was deemed "unkillable"—until he met Bekah. What started as a well-meaning birthday gift from a coworker ended in stem-wrenching tragedy.

A simple succulent no larger than the palm of her hand, Olivier didn't need much to survive. But Bekah, as usual, was ruthless. She placed him in a sterile cubicle—devoid of any natural light—and set a reminder to water him every week. Water him, she did.

Each Monday she assaulted Olivier with a monsoon-like deluge, drowning him so viciously he couldn't absorb the precious liquid fast enough. His weak, watery petals began detaching themselves out of sheer desperation, but this only seemed to anger her further. She upped the aquatic abuse to twice a week, his desperate cries for mercy all but ignored.

The tiny, owl-shaped pot that was his home is now filled with paperclips.

During our investigation, PNN received an anonymous tip that one of Bekah's early victims—

Edmund, a hanging English Ivy, had escaped. At the time of this report, he is the only known survivor. Today, Edmund shares a firsthand account of his time in Bekah's house of horrors.

*

Phil: Edmund, thank you for joining us.

Edmund: Thank you for having me. I feel very lucky to be here. What these old vines have witnessed is...barbaric.

Phil: I can't imagine how difficult it's been. Let's start at the beginning.

Edmund: About five seasons ago, I was plucked from the Home Depot Garden Center, handpicked by a woman named Dianne. She had a discerning eye and took her time choosing between us, running delicate fingers over our plump leaves. You could tell she had the nature of a plant lover.

Phil: Every houseplant's dream.

Edmund: I was thrilled to have been chosen, ready to thrive in my new home. I imagined sun-soaked days, surrounded by like-minded kin, Spider Plants and String-of-Pearls; Boston Ferns and Swiss Monsteras. Ah, the naivety of youth. Within a few hours, I was foisted into a barren third-floor studio apartment. No balcony, only a pair of small, south-facing windows. I realized then, Dianne was not destined to be my owner. I was nothing but an offering for her daughter, Bekah.

Phil: That must have been a shock.

Edmund: Most certainly. Phil, the woman didn't own a watering can. The day I arrived, I was thrust into a metal sink and drenched by a high-powered kitchen tap. Humiliating. After that, I sat on Bekah's breakfast bar, utterly unattended, without a sliver of daylight for more than ten days. I began to lose hope.

Then, to my surprise, Bekah crudely installed a hook in the popcorn ceiling near the window. Finally, I'd hang again, feel the warmth of the sun! But my excitement was short-lived—it took mere minutes for my weight to pull the hook free. I crashed to the ground and tumbled from my pot. One of my vines had been severed, my roots exposed, soil splayed over the linoleum. The carnage was gruesome. Two days later Bekah returned home and staged a halfhearted attempt to piece me back together. I've never been the same since.

Phil: I'm so sorry you had to go through that. Tell us a little about your escape.

Edmund: Frankly, Phil, it's a blur. In the weeks after the fall I was all but forgotten, left to wither in a dark corner next to the TV. My leaves were wilting, vines brittle from lack of moisture. It was difficult to think straight. I recall snippets of a conversation that day: *"I forgot that was tonight"* and *"shit, we're supposed to bring a gift?"* In my weakened state, I couldn't make sense of it.

The next thing I knew, I was whisked away. I was sure I was headed for the rubbish bin, but at that point I no longer feared death—life with Bekah was far worse. But the gracious frond of fate intervened.

That evening, I was presented to a lovely young woman, Eleanor, who saved my life. In fact, she has cared for me to this very day.

Phil: But your story doesn't end there. We've been told Eleanor lives in Bekah's apartment complex?

Edmund: That's correct. As Eleanor nursed me back to health, sunlight was paramount. She placed me near a window that provided a direct view into Bekah's apartment. While I was lucky enough to escape Bekah's clutches, I bore witness to so many others suffering at the hands of that monster. There were so many, Phil. Mummified corpses everywhere, scattered about like a macabre mausoleum. I've never seen such blind savagery. It's—it's still difficult to talk about.

Last year, I was relocated to Eleanor's bedroom, but the memories haunt me to this day. That woman deserves to pay for what she's done.

*

Despite our extensive investigation, Bekah's malicious motivations remain a mystery. But this story is not without hope. We have acquired evidence that Bekah recently spent $327.35 at World Market on plastic foliage replicas. We can only hope our artificial brethren have the fortitude to withstand the heartless fury of this unhinged menace.

Thank you for joining us for this PNN exclusive. This is Phil O'Dendron, wishing you, as always, health and hydration.

Ashleigh Adams is creative director and fiction writer. She tends to write about messy and complex female characters because she is one. Find her words in HAD, New Flash Fiction Review, Your Impossible Voice, Bath Flash Fiction, Sky Island Journal and JAKE, among others.

Follow her on Bluesky: @ashdoeswords or at ashleighadamswrites.com

Third Planet Government Agrees Historic Ban on Floppy Meat Production
by Emma Burnett

Thank you, Arrrkkkk-xxxs, for that riveting story.

Just today, the Third Planet Government announced a ban on the production and trade of floppy meat.

Native softshelled bipeds, affectionately known as 'floppies' by many, are considered by some *older* people to be a delicacy. Floppies were first discovered in the far northern reaches of the planet, living in small clusters along remnant landmasses near the pole. Although they showed some signs of intelligence, they were one of the few animals containing edible protein on the planet, and quickly became a staple of the original settlers' diets.

After the last of the ice caps melted to increase the planet's temperature to a more hospitable one, floppies were bred in climate-controlled farms. However, in recent decades, they have been increasingly kept as house pets. Floppies are capable of producing one to two offspring per year and can be reared in captivity to great effect.

The new law rolled out in phases, first banning floppy breeding and the running of abattoirs, then later banning the eating of floppies altogether. This has been described as a waste-prevention move by government officials, who say people should use up any frozen stores of floppy meat.

From the Third Planet Government headquarters, Krrrktt-xxk reports.

*

Thanks, Tskkk-kkktt.

I'm just outside the Third Planet Government headquarters on the First Floating Island. Originally designed by the first settlers, this island proudly displays our history. I scuttle past the oldest buildings, where chic restaurants proudly display sections of original colony ship panels. Beyond this, near the island's borders, are the last of the floppy farms, designed by our predecessors, who needed a stable source of meat, and where waste and offal could easily be offloaded into the water. As the floppy meat trade has died out—replaced by less contentious waterslimies farming—many of these have been converted into exclusive homes for wealthy residents.

The new law won't come into force for another decade, and will be rolled out in segments after that, with a ban first on older, more established floppies, followed by younger, and then infant floppy meat, which I'm told is the most tender and is the easiest to process. The Third Planet Government hopes this will give the supply chain enough time to transition to new enterprises. Support will be provided to help farmers and business owners make this shift.

Here, tucked behind the government buildings, is a traditional floppy meat restaurant, one of the few on the island. While these places are long gone from the main street, this restaurant has a pod of people waiting for a hole in their cosy location. Floppy meat can be prepared in a number of different ways, but this restaurant focuses on grilling, and is a firm favourite of older residents, who consider it a delicacy.

Over the past few centuries, floppy meat has become far less popular, with many younger people having never eaten it. Interviews with people about the governmental ban showed a stark generational divide.

I'm here with Tttsxxx-ttt, a local resident in their mid-300s, who clicks that they have been visiting the restaurant since they were a hatchling.

"We've eaten floppy meat since the settlers first arrived on the Third Planet. It's a cultural food. Why would you ban culture? You may as well tell us to leave the planet if we can't live freely."

A young octogenarian disagrees. "Lots of people keep floppies as pets today. Floppies are sweet, you know? And they're really smart. They can do tricks and things. They're like family, and it's really not very nice to eat your family."

Floppy meat consumption and production has been falling steadily for the past two centuries. Under the new law, those who farm, butcher, or sell floppy meat may be forced to serve up to 150 years doing hard labour in the asteroid belt. It won't actually be illegal to eat the meat, but it is hoped that the ban on rearing and sales will be enough to curb the practice.

The floppy meat industry has been very critical of the ban, arguing that the natural decline in floppy meat consumption should have been allowed to run its natural course.

A representative from the Native Animals Farmers' Union clicks: "Many people don't know what to do next. There are very few large animal species on the planet, and few as delicious as floppies. While we have been steadily moving towards relying on waterslimies for protein, the government shouldn't remove floppy meat from the market until we have fully transitioned. Removing employment from an entire sector can lead to unrest."

Ssxxxxkk-xxss took over their parents' floppy meat restaurant. When asked how the ban will impact them, they click in dismay.

"I don't know what I'll do. My whole business relies on floppy meat. I don't think they should close us down, I think they should just improve the conditions of floppies raised for consumption, and the slaughtering process. It's not just about removing their voiceboxes so they're not so noisy. We should also make sure that the farms are hygienic and humane."

In contrast to this, floppy rights organisations are in full support of the forthcoming ban, many saying that it should be rolled out sooner, and in one go, rather than in stages. Kktttkk-xxt from the Floppy Protection Society is a long-time campaigner for floppies.

"I'm thrilled that this ban has been passed by the Third Planet Government. We need to move towards better treatment of animals, and this is a major step in the right direction. Next, we need to petition to stop the cruel practice of surgically muting the floppies."

There has been no word so far about public protest against the ban, but with emotions running high, people may be scuttling en masse soon.

That was Krrrktt-xxk reporting from First Floating Island. Stay tuned for the next episode in our continuing drama, Clicking Across the Universe.

Emma Burnett is a researcher and writer. She has had stories in Grimdark Magazine, Nature:Futures, Mythaxis, Northern Gravy, Radon, Uncharted, Flash Fiction Online, Apex, MetaStellar, The Forge, and more. She's pretty excited that her first book, Ex Partum, will be released in June 2026 by Atthis Arts.

You can find Emma @slashnburnett.bsky.social or emmaburnett.uk.

A Foofaraw on Mahiladū Station
by Joel Glover

"I think you're going to have to explain this to me again."

Zetna had a hangover. It was, by her reckoning, somewhere around three steps short of moving from an indefinite article to a definite article. From *a* hangover to *the* hangover.

Her office was full.

Overfull.

Mahiladū Station had no real gaol or holding cells, so her office would have to serve. Men were cable-tied to benches and chairs. The room reeked of sweat, beers, and antiseptic. The medical tinge was being added by the liniments smeared across cuts and bruises sufficient to fill an infirmary ward. According to the information on her data slate the infirmary was also full.

"That fucking idiot said that Nelson Nkrumah was the greatest basketball player of all time."

The large man shackled to the chair opposite her pointed his scarred index finger at an equally large man shackled to a bench on the other side of the room. The main thing that differentiated the pair was their beards. The face opposite her was completely covered in hair, except for spots where henna red hair had been chafed away by a breathing apparatus. The man he was accusing of being a 'fucking idiot' was sporting a similar, but undyed, length of hair.

"Because he fucking is!" retorted blackbeard.

"I can't believe it! This fucking guy! Still with the same stupid shit!"

The men leaned towards each other, adding spittle to the volume of their argument.

Zetna placed her forehead on the cool plastic of the desk and closed her eyes. Her hope was that when she opened them again she would have dragged herself from this nightmare into a waking world which was at least quieter.

She had no such luck.

"I ain't about to hear no slander against LeBron!"

Redbeard was still shouting.

"The man played until he was forty-seven years old, in the toughest era of the NBA."

"As a bit player for a decade, just to keep his son in the league," a skinny man shouted from across the room.

Red continued as if he hadn't registered the complaint.

"He was a twenty-one time NBA All Star, seven time NBA champion, *still* the NBA's all-time leading point scorer, *still* second all-time in assists!"

These facts were recited with religious fervour, chanted like a mantra.

"NBA, NBA, NBA," blackbeard replied, each repetition more seasoned with the flavours of the language of his childhood. "Nobody cares about NBA. The world is bigger than NBA my friend. The game is bigger than NBA. Nelson Nkrumah is the greatest shooter the game has ever seen. 48.3% from beyond the 3, 19.2% from the logo!"

"Gravity assisted shooting," redbeard sneered. "He's playing in 0.97% Earth Standard Gravity, he grew up in a gravity well where he could grow to 2.4 metres unencumbered. Plus he's using Cavendish Tech growth hormones. You can't trust any stats after the introduction of crab gene tweaking. The last true shooter in basketball was Double Double."

"Double Double. Typical French arrogance," blackbeard coughed.

Beyond the arguing pair, the ripples of discussion had been picking up again, like the echoes of far-off thunder above the seas of her homeworld Chetlat. The invocation of whatever Double Double was made the stormfronts collide. One fat man headbutted another fat man in the face, splitting his nose, spilling blood all over her previously very neat filing system. As the pair were chained to the same bench, retribution was immediate and commensurate with the original attack and suddenly there were two men bleeding on her floor.

At the very rear of the room, a shockingly large man stood with a roar, tearing his leg from the chair he was sitting on with a spasmodic lunge. The plastic of the zip-ties shredded under the pressure from his massive muscles. Suddenly free, he began to lay about men on the other side of the argument to him with his new cudgel.

"Oh for fuck's sake," groaned Zeta.

The pacification grenade in her desk drawer was there for emergencies only. That an argument about basketball had turned into an emergency was beyond any expectation Zetna had when she secreted it there.

She took her last deep breath of untainted station air, sour with sweat and the copper tang of blood, then thumbed the activation trigger.

Pink mist filled the room, coiling into unwary nostrils, stealing sense and sensibility from everybody in the room.

She would run up the three steps between *a* hangover to *the* hangover because of this, and take more steps beyond.

What a day.

Joel has the hands and feet of a much taller man. His short fiction publications include pieces in the Space Wizard Science Fantasy anthology "Where No Man Has Gone Before," the Air and Nothingness collection "Our Dust Earth," Nature:Futures, "Big Smoke Pulp vol 1", Pulp Lit Mag, Wensum Lit, Altered Reality, and foofaraw. Grimdark Magazine described his self-published debut as "tantalisingly dark and brutal." He has four series of fantasy novels he is eager for you to read.

The 5-Star Intergalactic Telephone Company
by E.J. LeRoy

I was not looking forward to making this call. Let's just say there's a reason why the 5-Star Intergalactic Telephone Company has a reputation for being one of the worst telecommunication corporations this side of the Milky Way. But I couldn't afford their lousy service any longer. And I sure wasn't going to pay for this month's phony charges—among them a call to a mattress company five planets away, three calls to a planet I've never even heard of, and seven calls to something called "Triple Babes from Tibah," which suspiciously cost 4.99 CSD (Colony Seven Dollars) per minute.

Already, I had been on hold for over an hour, stuck in my chair listening to horrendous hold music seemingly designed to destroy my eardrums. Whoever thought the not-so-soothing sounds of Anghartian dragons snoring constituted music needed an immediate cranial exam, not to mention a hearing test. I would have passed the time playing on my computer if my internet access hadn't been mysteriously disconnected a few hours earlier. I know I paid the bill, but that's another story entirely.

"5-Star Intergalactic Telephone Company," someone finally said on the other end.

Whoever it was sounded eerily similar to my third-grade teacher, Miss Harris, who was about a hundred years old at the time, had a hairy mole, and wore bright red lipstick that looked like blood she probably sucked from misbehaving students. According to the official story, troublemaker Riley Becker disappeared one day because his parents got transferred, but I never believed it. The last thing Miss Harris ever said to Riley was, "Young man, I'll see you in detention." I doubt he ever made it that far. Miss Harris looked surprisingly refreshed the next day in class, and Riley was never seen again. You can guess why. People think my theory is nuts, but it's yet to be refuted.

"Yeah, uh, hi," I said to Not-Miss-Harris. "I need to cancel my subscription to—"

"Oh, I'm afraid that's not possible this time of year," Not-Miss-Harris interrupted. "Contracts, you know."

"I don't have a contract," I said quickly. "I'm on a monthly subscription plan and—"

"In that case, why do you wish to cancel your subscription? The 5-Star Intergalactic Telephone Company offers the best off-planet telecommunication service in the galaxy." Not-Miss-Harris continued in this manner, obviously reading from a script. She didn't give me a chance to interrupt and punctuated each sentence with a loud snap, almost like she was chewing gum. She probably *was* chewing gum. Either that or she was a species with perpetually puckered lips. I remember my first encounter with that kind of alien. She looked like a green octopus with suckers for lips. When my roommate at the time dared me to kiss her, I stupidly did it. To make a long story short, we both had to be rushed to the hospital to keep my mouth from being ripped off. Needless to say, the guy who pulled that prank on me is no longer my roommate. And if he's the one behind the "Triple Babes from Tibah" charges on my phone bill, I won't be held responsible for giving him three well-deserved black eyes.

The prattling on the other end of the phone finally stopped. Before I could say anything, I heard, "Are you still there, miss?"

"Mister," I corrected. Mother of Kalujulah, did I really sound like a woman over the phone? It wasn't the first time I was mistaken for the opposite sex either. I remember a similar incident from two years ago when my boss and I had to meet an off-planet CEO who had come to our laboratory to discuss a potential partnership. He was a nice guy, or so I thought. When I gave him a tour of the laboratory and the rest of the business, he was *very* friendly and went so far as to invite me to dinner. It was only near the end of the tour that it somehow came out that he thought I was a woman the entire time. In all fairness to the CEO, he came from a planet where the men are hairless and the women would put a wooly mammoth to shame. When he saw my long hair—not even a beard, mind you—he concluded I was a woman and became smitten with me. Furious about my supposed deception, the CEO stormed off, the business deal didn't go through, and I didn't get any dinner.

"Please explain why you wish to cancel your subscription," Not-Miss-Harris said. "Here at the 5-Star Intergalactic Telephone Company, we pride ourselves in offering the best telecommunication service in the galaxy." Kalujulah, help me; the script had started again! This time, I had to stop it before I lost even more brain cells than had already evaporated.

"Yeah, about that," I started. Not-Miss-Harris just kept talking over me. She didn't stop until she reached the end of the script. Then there was a sweet moment of silence I knew I had to capitalize on. "Listen," I said, "I need to cancel my subscription because of the price and—"

"If you are concerned about the price, then we have a special offer for you!" Here came the script again. This time, a few sentences about current package deals were added. This was the kind of torture you only heard about on Planet Anghart. Their chief torturer is rumored to have killed one of his enemies simply by talking him to death. I never believed it before, but the story was becoming increasingly plausible.

"No, no specials!" I blurted out. "Look, there are a bunch of false charges on my bill and—"

"Well, why didn't you say so? Here at the 5-Star Intergalactic Telephone Company, we take erroneous charges very seriously. We pride ourselves—"

"Yes, I know. Can we just take care of the phony charges first, and then take care of the cancellation?"

"I would be glad to help you look over your telephone bill. And when we take care of any problems here at the 5-Star Intergalactic Telephone Company, we hope a cancellation will not be necessary." I was not about to tell Not-Miss-Harris that I was going to cancel my subscription regardless, if only because I never wanted to hear the phrase, "Here at the 5-Star Intergalactic Telephone Company," ever again.

"Will you please give me your name and account number?"

Finally, we were getting somewhere! "I'm Jeff Stark. My account's under the name Jeffrey Stark. And my account number is—"

"Wait, are you *the* Jeff Stark?" Was it possible that Not-Miss-Harris had somehow heard about the Our Solutions Laboratory fiasco? There was no way I was going to live this down. No matter what happened, I needed to stay calm and collected.

"I'm *a* Jeff Stark." That didn't sound too incriminating, I hoped.

"But are you *the* Jeff Stark?" She knew, didn't she? This was not good.

"Um..."

"I'm a huge fan of your work, Mr. Stark," Not-Miss-Harris gushed. "I especially loved 'Laboratory at Midnight.'"

Laboratory at Midnight? Was that what they were calling the incident now? When I accidentally blew up the lab while testing flame-retardant vintage disco costumes, it couldn't have been later than 10:00 PM. As for the costumes, they were about the only thing that survived the explosion. If I hadn't been wearing one of them, that probably would have been the end of me, and I wouldn't be having this ridiculous conversation. As for why I was wearing one of the vintage disco costumes... my family's lawyer strongly advised me not to divulge that information. Anyway, I don't really remember, but whatever reason I had seemed important at the time.

"You are so fortunate to be so accomplished," Not-Miss-Harris continued.

"Well, I wouldn't call it an accomplishment, exactly..."

"Nonsense! Your work as an essayist, screenwriter, actor, director, and former adult film star is well-known throughout the galaxy."

"Former adult film star?" I said, dumbfounded. For a brief moment, the case of mistaken identity was oddly flattering. And it was a good thing I didn't say anything about the laboratory incident. "Yeah, uh, that's not me," I admitted. "I'm just plain old Jeff Stark." I stopped myself from saying I was a former employee of Our Solutions Corporation in case Not-Miss-Harris figured out who I really was.

"Oh, I apologize for the misunderstanding. Here at the 5-Star Intergalactic Telephone Company, we strive to provide..."

Oh, Kalujulah, make it stop! I interrupted her with my account number, which actually made her stop talking and making smacking sounds. Then there was the sound of typing, a sign of progress.

"Very good, Mr. Stark," Not-Miss-Harris said. "I have your account information here. Everything looks like it's in order."

"But it's not in order," I said. "I never called this mattress store in…" I tried to sound out the name of the planet that had too many "k's," "x's," and "z's" than should have been possible to pronounce.

"Xixakilkazez," Not-Miss-Harris supplied helpfully.

"Uh, yeah, that planet. And I never called any of these other planets on the list either. And I certainly didn't call 'Triple Babes from Tibah,' whatever that is." I could certainly guess what "Triple Babes from Tibah" was, especially considering the charge was nearly 5 CSD per minute, but it didn't hurt to pretend to be completely ignorant. Although, as my lawyer informed me regarding the laboratory incident, ignorance was not a valid argument. The only reason charges weren't pressed was because the investigation revealed my boss was going to burn the business down anyway to collect the insurance. I had accidentally saved him the trouble, but they caught him anyway. They also said my boss had allegedly sabotaged my work, causing the explosion to occur. Sure, let's go with that.

"I'm sorry, Mr. Stark, but each of these phone calls was made from your telephone number."

"But they're all mistakes!" I said. "I haven't even heard of most of the planets and businesses listed. How could I have called them?"

"If you are dissatisfied with your service here at the 5-Star Intergalactic Telephone Company, we would be pleased to run a complete investigation on your behalf at no charge to you. Simply pay the bill that was sent to you, and we will refund you for any erroneous charges."

"I'm not going to pay for calls I didn't make. Let me speak with your supervisor."

"I'm terribly sorry, Mr. Stark, but my supervisor is currently out of the office on a business trip off-planet."

"How convenient."

"Mr. Stark."

Uh-oh, I thought. Not-Miss-Harris was using Miss Harris's teacher tone with me. It was the disappearance of Riley Becker all over again.

"Here at the 5-Star Intergalactic Telephone Company," Not-Miss-Harris continued, "we take our investigations very seriously and ask only for your cooperation as one of our valued and loyal customers. Because at the 5-Star Intergalactic Telephone Company, we put customers first and foremost..."

Was Not-Miss-Harris's droning, bureaucratic form of customer service supposed to be my punishment for accidentally blowing up a laboratory? If listening to this nonsense a minute longer was an official judiciary sentence, I would sue on the grounds of cruel and unusual punishment. That is, I *would* sue if I wasn't currently jobless and scrambling to find another source of income. It isn't exactly easy to find a new job when "caused a laboratory explosion" is on your résumé.

"I'm not going to be a customer much longer," I said when Not-Miss-Harris finally stopped talking.

"Mr. Stark, we take customer retention seriously here at the 5-Star Intergalactic Telephone Company. If you pay for the charges listed on your bill, we will give you intergalactic telephone service free of charge for the next three months."

The ridiculous charges on my telephone bill amounted to more than three months of service and Not-Miss-Harris knew it. I called her bluff and told her so. She was not deterred.

"In that case, Mr. Stark, we will give you six months of free service covering our entire intergalactic network."

"Yeah, but I don't want to continue my subscription to the 5-Star Intergalactic Telephone Company. I just want to have the bad charges cleared and cancel my subscription. That's all!"

"I'm afraid it doesn't work that way, Mr. Stark." Not-Miss-Harris punctuated the end of her sentence with another loud snap. "You see, Mr. Stark, according to your account information, you live in a remote area on Colony Seven. Without the 5-Star Intergalactic Telephone Company, you would be unable to make off-planet telephone calls. And I know from your records that you frequently call Planet Jelipa. The only other way you could continue to make these calls is by purchasing an expensive by-the-minute phone plan from an inferior competitor. So, as you see, Mr. Stark, here at the 5-Star Intergalactic Telephone Company, we are looking out for your best interests as a loyal and valued customer."

"Ending intergalactic telephone service is fine by me," I said. "I don't need to call Planet Jelipa anymore."

"And why is that?"

"I don't think that's any of your business."

"Mr. Stark, in order to best serve our customers here at the 5-Star Intergalactic Telephone Company, it is imperative that we fully understand why our loyal and valued clients feel the need to cancel their subscriptions."

"My brother no longer lives off-planet," I said, just to shut her up. Greg was, in fact, the only reason I had this awful 5-Star Intergalactic Telephone Company service in the first place. As a political science major, my brother attended school off-planet and had to travel around the galaxy as part of his education. That's where the intergalactic telephone service came in, so I could talk to him when he lived on Jelipa. Then, when he graduated, I needed to keep the service because he was stationed at some obscure diplomatic post on another planet in the middle of nowhere. But ever since the diplomatic incident on Planet Tanghira, which happened only days after my laboratory accident, any need for intergalactic telephone service disappeared. Rather, the need for intergalactic telephone service crashed and burned along with Greg's short-lived political career.

"Surely you have other relatives and friends living off-planet you want to keep in touch with," Not-Miss-Harris persisted.

"No, I don't." Greg really was the only reason I ever got entangled with the 5-Star Intergalactic Telephone Company. Seriously. Everyone else in my family lived—and still lives—on Colony Seven, so I constantly got to hear over the local phone system about what a screw-up I was while my petted older brother was off solving intergalactic diplomatic crises. Maybe I shouldn't gloat about his inglorious downfall, but it's hard not to.

On his last diplomatic mission, he was supposed to greet an official from the Planet Tanghira. Of course, on Tanghira, they speak Tanghiri, which is damned near impossible for any human to speak. So, when Greg was supposed to greet the official and address him as, "Your Excellence," he accidentally called him, "Your Flatulence." That would have been bad enough, but Tanghira has a dueling culture. So, having insulted and humiliated the official in front of his entire cabinet, Greg was called out for a duel, which under their laws he couldn't refuse. I don't know if they copied old Earth books and movies, but apparently, they have those old-fashioned duels with pistols—ten paces apart and the whole bit.

So, there was Greg, back-to-back with the official he had accidentally called "Your Flatulence," ready to shoot or be shot for that faux pas. Then some other guy started to count to ten. Of course, Greg, having a hard time with the language like pretty much any human, and being understandably nervous as hell about the prospect of being shot, misheard the numbers. At the count of "ten," which Greg misheard as "nine" in their language, the official turned around, but Greg didn't, causing him to be shot squarely in the butt. By that planet's screwy laws, honor was served, and Greg was returned home to our fussing parents and my well-deserved ribbing. Hey, I may have blown up a laboratory while dressed in a flame-retardant vintage disco costume, but at least I've never caused an intergalactic diplomatic crisis that ended with being shot in the ass. I'm just saying.

"Mr. Stark," Not-Miss-Harris said, "I urge you to reconsider cancelling your subscription with the 5-Star Intergalactic Telephone Company."

"I'm not reconsidering," I said. My local phone service would do just fine now to continue calling my brother to let him know how happy I am that I'm no longer the only screw-up in the family.

"Very well, Mr. Stark. If you keep your subscription with the 5-Star Intergalactic Telephone Company, we will remove your charges for this month and give you a new package deal for a year."

"No deal," I said. "I'm only asking you to erase all the charges and cancel my subscription. I'm not interested in doing business with the 5-Star Intergalactic Telephone Company any longer. I mean it."

There was a long silence, followed by a few thoughtful smacking sounds. "Are you certain there is nothing we can do to retain you as a customer, Mr. Stark?"

"Nothing at all."

"Fine, you're cancelled. You'll receive confirmation by e-mail. Click it and you're through." Then Not-Miss-Harris hung up. Apparently, I wasn't such a valued customer after all. But at least after two hours of agony, I was finally free of the 5-Star Intergalactic Telephone Company. All I had to do was confirm the cancellation by e-mail. But when I logged into my computer, the internet was still down.

"Great!" I said aloud. "Just great!" When I found the internet customer service number in my computer files, I felt like punching the monitor. Intergalactic Internet Plus was a subsidiary of the 5-Star Intergalactic Telephone Company, and the phone number for customer service was the same.

"All right, Not-Miss-Harris," I said, dialing the number, "I'm ready for Round 2." And, just to add to all my life's disappointments, the damn phone didn't work.

E.J. LeRoy is a Pushcart Prize nominated writer whose work has appeared in several publications including After the Storm Magazine, Cetera Magazine, Neon Dystopia, NonBinary Review, and Tales from the Crosstimbers. LeRoy also has a science fiction mpreg novella published by The Whumpy Printing Press.

Visit the author's website at http://ejleroy.weebly.com.

The Anchorite
by Stuart Docherty

The priest met me at the doorway to the church and handed me a towel. It was raining heavily and even though I had only run the short distance from the car park, I was dripping wet.

"Do, please, come this way, away from the cold," the priest said, gathering his robes about him. "The Anchorite is below. He will offer you counsel, though remember his answers are not always comforting, nor easily understood. Wisdom is rarely easy to digest." We passed through the nave and lightning flashed through the windows. I bowed my head as we passed before the altar, and the priest led me through a low door that went down to the basement.

The basement was dank and gloomy, and I could hear water dripping from somewhere. A thin cable ran along the ceiling and some old lightbulbs shone weakly down the narrow corridor in front of me. I had to crouch a little as the ceiling was so low. There was the musky smell of old books and forgotten wisdom as our footsteps echoed down the hall. When we stopped in front of a sealed door, I figured we were just about below the altar. Beside the door was a small opening in the masonry that revealed the room on the other side. I looked to the priest, who simply smiled and nodded towards the opening.

Through the gap, a man's face appeared. The room on the other side was lit by candlelight and it was hard to make out his features, but he was well into middle age. His hair was long and rangy, and a similar beard grew to cover most of the features of his face.

"Well then," the man said. "Ask your questions and leave me to my studies."

"Ahh, I see," I said. "It's one of those stories."

The Anchorite's eyes flicked towards the priest.

"The author's just using this anchorite as a symbol, like most of his writing," I continued. "Maybe there's some deeper meaning behind it, maybe not. It's hard to say with this stuff. He always puts the subtext ahead of the text. Symbols are more important than the plot."

"Waste not my time," the Anchorite intoned, a boom of thunder followed his words. There must have been some sort of hagioscope in the room, a clear line of sight to the altar, for the Anchorite looked up and began mumbling a prayer where I thought the altar was.

"I bet he started this with some sort of weather feature. It'll end like that, too. Maybe you're realising it now, but there isn't really a strong plot holding all of this together. There'll be *something*—some sort of escalation to keep you interested, though. You might think it's some sort of deeper artistic work, and maybe it is. But could you really tell if it wasn't?"

"Are... are you quite alright?" the priest asked, placing a hand on my shoulder. He looked through the small window towards the Anchorite; both their faces were pained. I smiled at them both in turn.

"The author took up writing because he likes to read, but he finds the whole business of construction really quite difficult. It's why he often uses symbols that don't quite mesh together, like priests. Sure, if you ask him, he'll tell you the real value in fiction comes from that mystical, sublime experience that some great writers are able to achieve. But deep down, if you got the truth out of him, he'd say it's mostly about set and setting. You only get to that 'divine experience' through preparation and ritual."

Through the small window, the Anchorite turned. He disappeared from view for a moment and then returned, his eyes wide.

"Father," he said, "you've got to do something about that leak. It's coming in now, the rain. Take this charlatan away."

On cue, a drop of water fell from the ceiling onto my head. I looked down the corridor, and saw it falling through other gaps in the masonry. At the far end, it started to sit, building into a puddle.

"The point is," I said, "although he's trying to guide you towards that revelation, he's just doing it by imitating, or copying (depending on how strict your definition is) other writers. He can only admit he doesn't know what he's doing in that self-satisfied, smug way, and puts value on intuition because it's largely untraceable."

The water continued to eke through the stonework and rose to my ankles.

"I really think we ought to leave," the priest said, tugging on my sleeve.

"Aye father, and don't forget about me." The Anchorite's voice echoed through the little opening and seemed very far away.

I pulled my sleeve away from the priest. "You've got to consider what's really best for him. Sure, there's a chance he'll churn out something wonderful if he keeps at it. But there's also a probability that he'll squander his life writing these inane little stories trying to 'touch the divine' or something like that."

The water had risen to my waist and the priest was scrambling at his belt for the key to the Anchorite's cell. The Anchorite banged against the door and the water started to run through the squint. The light through the squint disappeared.

"Sometimes it's best to be truthful, to really let someone know what's good for them. Sometimes it's the worst thing you can do. Whatever you do, *do something*." The water was up to my shoulders, and I had to angle my face towards the heavens. The priest was wading through the water behind me, but the rain started to rush down the stairs, creating a current that the father couldn't contend with. When the priest lost his footing and fell beneath the swirling waters, the lights blinked out, leaving us in darkness.

Stuart is a British writer and poet based in Tokyo, where he writes, eats too much, and pretends to speak Japanese. You can find his work at ergot., Maudlin House, and 7th Circle Pyrite.

The Final Test
by E. Florian Gludovacz

He stared intently at the bottle on the table in front of him. A single wine bottle, dark green and full, uncorked and aerating, the cork placed on a neat little plain white plate, ready for his examination. Next to it stood a single long-stemmed wine glass, the curvature reflecting the afternoon daylight and spreading a hypnotic puddle of light onto the stark white tablecloth.

This was it! This was the moment that would decide the future; the rest of his life. Jonathan took a deep, calming breath and looked up at the assembled personages in front of him. The board that was going to judge him was comprised of four people. There was the Nervous Nelly, the Acerbic Asshole, the Bitter Bastard, and finally, the Sour Bitch. They all had names, of course, but Jon had not paid any attention when they introduced themselves. He did this frequently, not paying attention to people's names. He just didn't care who they were on a personal level. Instead he labelled them according to their looks, their demeanour, their attitudes.

"...and so, the practical part of the examination will entail tasting a single bottle of wine. Why, you ask? Well, at this advanced level, there is no point in a whole series of tastings. Everybody who has made it this far, Mr. Willis, will be able to identify most of the wines placed in front of them. Multiple wines would just blur the success rate through the law of averages. Statistics and all that. I'm sure you understand," the Nervous Nelly said in his thin, high-pitched voice that grated on Jon's nerves already. "I'm sure you realize this is the only fair test we can administer. In the past fifty-four years fewer than three hundred applicants have successfully tested to attain the rank of Master Sommelier."

Jon's lips twisted into a wry little smile as he nodded his understanding. He didn't need their pompous explanations. He was the youngest applicant ever to make it here. And the thing was, in a very real way, he didn't even care. He wasn't a dried-up snob like these people were. He just loved wine. He enjoyed drinking it—sometimes a little too much —as the hangovers after a weekend binge attested to. He liked talking about wine, he enjoyed learning about it, he loved the process that went into it all: the vineyards, the cellars, the barrels, large and small. The blending of wines, the character of varietals, but most of all he loved the scent and taste of wine. The fact of the matter, though, was that he was actually very good at it, and had been able to make a career out of wine. He had studied, had taken all the relevant exams, and had worked diligently to become the best sommelier the world had ever seen. He despised the people in front of him, yet at the same time, he craved their admiration and acceptance. These were the only people in the entire world who might understand some aspects of what went on in his mind.

"...so if you're ready, I'll pour, and we can commence the test," the Bitter Bastard droned.

"Yes, thank you. I'm ready."

He watched the fat, bald man handle the bottle carefully and then pour a small measure into the glass. The color was lighter than he had expected. This was no ancient vintage, cloudy with age and the processes of maturation.

Interesting!

He picked up the cork carefully, examined it for any signs of potassium bitartrate, depth of penetration of the wine into the cork, general color of the residue on the cork, and gave it a delicate sniff. The cork was neutral with just a hint of the wine blending into the musty natural notes. So far, so good. He stepped back and eyed the glass critically before picking it up by the stem, holding it against the light to admire the rich tones of the liquid. It was a full garnet, with slight ruby undertones, and a translucent quality along the wall of the glass, where he noticed a light brown tinge. He tilted the glass gently, began swirling it around, then stared at it intently. There it was! The slow separation of the alcohol from the rest of the wine. The alcohol ran down the inside of the glass in slow, thick runnels, spreading out as gravity took hold of the elixir and drew it back down into the wine.

This was strong stuff. Well over fourteen percent. Possibly closer to fifteen. Well, that ruled out a number of varietals already. Along with the color and the age, he formed an opinion.

The Sour Bitch watched him impatiently, but had the professional good grace not to fidget. He hated when people did that. Some did it out of ignorance, some—mostly professionals—out of conscious or sublimated spite. But it didn't really matter; he was about to taste the wine. He lifted the glass reverently, slowly to his face and sniffed gently, then inhaled deeply after another moment. It was fruity, alcohol-forward, as he expected. There was a hint of spice, some acidity, a suggestion of cherry.

Jon smiled and put the glass to his lips, taking a small sip and letting the glorious liquid roll across his tongue in a gentle caress. He took another sip and drew air through his lips, aerating the wine and releasing more of the flavour into his sinuses. Yes, the alcohol content played into the flavour, releasing the lighter, etheric aromas. You couldn't have proper wine below thirteen percent, he thought to himself for the millionth time. You just didn't get the subtlety with weak wines. He made chewing motions, swirling the wine around his mouth, and finally stepped to the side of the table where the spit bucket awaited.

Fuck it!

He swallowed the wine and smiled at the examiners. The Nervous Nelly appeared almost shocked, while the Acerbic Asshole made a disgusted face. Interestingly, the other two did not react at all. Well, it wasn't against the rules to swallow instead of spitting the wine into the vessel, but these professionals obviously had their own preferences.

He didn't care. He was only tasting this one wine, so they could all go to hell as far as he was concerned. He enjoyed drinking and that was that.

They stared at him expectantly now.

He let them wait another twenty seconds and then began.

"Interesting selection. I'd say this is a Sangiovese, what with the high alcohol content, the high acidity, and the sour cherry notes. There are earthy tones and a slightly above-medium level of tannin in the mix," he paused, considering for a moment. None of the examiners betrayed any outward reactions at all. That in itself was telling, he thought. "As far as terroir is concerned, I am reminded of something like a Rhône Valley appellation..."

"That's your answer?" the Sour Bitch interjected, a note of triumph creeping into her voice.

"Hardly," Jon scoffed. "I am merely observing an interesting parallel. The flavour reminds me of that region, but it is definitely not a French wine. Now, what would be reminiscent of the Rhône region, while being from somewhere else?" He paused dramatically, letting the tension build, for he knew that his examiners—and perhaps tormentors—were just as nervous as he was, albeit for different reasons. He knew the Sour Bitch and the Bitter

Bastard did not personally like him and hoped he would fail.

"No, we are considering a region that receives coastal winds similar to the mistral, that deals with regular daily shifts in temperature, and has a hard, mineral soil. I think the only region that fits all of those criteria would be Southern California!"

Again he paused to let his words sink in. They were impressed with him now, he noted.

"Specifically, I think we are dealing with the Temecula appellation. I'd go so far as to say that it is from the Mountain Vineyards Estate. And the vintage has to be 2018."

He picked up the glass and drank the remaining wine in one gulp, then set the glass down.

There! He had made his statement and hoped it would be good enough. He knew he was right, of course, but would his presentation impress his judges sufficiently?

"Well done, Mr. Willis!" the Nervous Nelly exclaimed. "That was very impressive and absolutely correct."

The Sour Bitch made a sour face and the Bitter Bastard sighed.

"Now that we are done with the practical part of the examination, it's time to move on to a bit of theory for the final part of the exam," the Acerbic Asshole said, and smiled as he continued. "You will have to answer every question correctly in order to pass and I can assure you that you will need all of your wits about you." He glanced meaningfully at the spit bucket.

"I'm ready."

"Your final theoretical examination will be in wine-pairings," the Sour Bitch gloated. "We realise that it's a field that is open to some interpretation, so you better make your opinions very convincing."

"And they better not be by rote," the Bitter Bastard added with a vicious undertone. "You will have to come up with some original thinking."

"Are you ready, Mr. Willis?" the Nervous Nelly asked.

"I am."

"Good, because we will now ask you for four wine pairing recommendations," the Acerbic Asshole grinned. "You will recommend the most suitable wine for a number of global catastrophes and disasters!"

"First," the Nervous Nelly whined. "Which wine would you recommend for a nuclear catastrophe?"

"Petite Syrah, of course," Jon shot back.

"Why?" the Acerbic Asshole retorted. "You'll have to come up with a very convincing reason. Just spitting out the first wine that comes to mind will not do."

"I was just about to elaborate, before I was interrupted," he replied with an easy, almost insolent smile. "Petite Syrah is a rich and heavy wine that is well known for its full body and flavour, particularly for its rich, velvety tannins that coat the tongue as you drink it. If I were inside the blast radius of an atomic disaster, I'd want a rich, luscious wine before the radiation sickness kicks in. With blood running out of your orifices and boils all over your body, I don't think light and fruity is going to cut it, do you?"

They looked at each other, the Nervous Nelly whispered something into the Acerbic Asshole's ear, and then they all nodded with various degrees of reluctance.

"That's a rather convincing argument you make there, Mr. Willis," the Bitter Bastard conceded. "We really cannot fault your logic. Petite Syrah is indeed a perfect pairing to a nuclear meltdown. But there's no time to rest on your laurels! Instead, tell me, what would pair well with a major flooding event?"

"Zweigelt. I'm sure you are familiar with the grape. It's a fairly recently developed variety from Austria that is incredibly versatile. It works well in mass production, but can also hold its own against any grape when fermented in small-batch barrique barrels. The region around Rust in the Burgenland springs to mind for the latter. However, the reason I'd recommend Zweigelt in connection with flooding is that it is frequently served with water as a Spritzer in summer. It will hold its character and bouquet reasonably well even in its watered-down state, so I am convinced that it is the perfect wine to drink during a flood."

They went into a brief huddle before turning back to him.

"Again, you are correct," the Acerbic Asshole stated in clipped tones. "Now what pairs with climate change?"

"Barolo."

Jon noticed an involuntary narrowing of the Sour Bitch's eyes and knew that he was on the right track. He continued.

"Climate change is a slow catastrophe. Unlike the previous situations, you don't have to make any snap judgements. You have time to consider and make the best of the situation. We all know that Barolo is a wine that matures slowly and ages well. So, if you lay in an ample supply of Barolo in time, you are in a good position to enjoy both your wine and the climate change for years to come."

This time the examiners only exchanged a brief glance before the Sour Bitch spoke up.

"Indeed. You are absolutely correct, Mr. Willis. However, I can't help but notice that so far you have only suggested pairings involving red wine. Are you in any way averse to a white wine?"

"Not at all. Actually, quite the contrary is true. However, so far you have only given me red wine catastrophes, so don't blame me if I don't offer any white wine pairings."

"You are correct," she admitted. "But now tell me what to pair with a tornado!"

"Sauvignon Blanc."

"Are you certain?"

"Of course I am. It's a light, crisp, and refreshing wine that has invigorating notes of tropical fruit, citrus, and lemongrass. If you are trying to outrun a storm or take shelter in a bunker, you don't want to be weighed down by some heavy vintage. I'd especially recommend a New Zealand South Island from the Marlborough region. Their wines embody some of the finest features of the varietal. It's like sunshine in a bottle, so it's just what you want to be drinking during a tornado."

His examiners went into another huddle, this time whispering quite vehemently and obviously arguing among themselves. The Sour Bitch made some wild, intense hand gestures, but finally relented. Jon could watch her deflate right in front of his eyes as she turned back to him.

"I have to admit that you are correct once more. I don't have anything to add to your recommendation."

"Congratulations, Mr. Willis! You have passed the final examination and are now a member of the select elite of Master Sommeliers!" the Nervous Nelly exclaimed and took his hand to shake it vigorously.

"Well done," the Bitter Bastard said with a shrug and gave Jon a pat on the shoulder.

"That wasn't too shabby," the Acerbic Asshole said, shaking his hand almost warmly.

"I hate to admit it, but you are good," the Sour Bitch admitted.

"Thank you all," Jon smiled modestly. He went to the table, picked up the Sangiovese and the glass, poured a good measure, and drank it with gusto.

They gaped at him. This was not the decorous behaviour they were used to.

"What are your plans for the future, now that you are a Master Sommelier?" she asked.

"I'm going to go home, open a bottle of wine, and get roaringly drunk," he grinned. "And before you ask, it will be Primitivo!"

"Why?"

"Because I like the word!" he said as he strode through the door, leaving the pathetic quartet behind.

E. Florian Gludovacz has been a writer, musician, and artist since his teens. He was born in Austria and grew up living in different parts of Europe (Germany, France, the UK, and Austria). He currently resides in rural Southern California with his wife and their mixed Great Pyrenean Mountain Dog. He has been known to enjoy the occasional glass of wine.

His stories have appeared online and in print in numerous publications including "Cosmic Roots and Eldritch Shores", "foofaraw", Fission #5 (BSFA), "To the Dogs" anthology (Altitude Press), "Midnight Menagerie" anthology (WolfSinger Publications), as well as the "Consumed" anthology (Arbutus Films).

He is a finalist for the 2025 WSFA Small Press Award.

In the Thick of Time
by B. Morris Allen

Time was uninterrupted. It extended down the hill in one direction, while in the other it was lost amid a line of septs that streamed down like ants. The septs were brief, momentary, clans stretching across a handful of generations at best. They faded in and out, overlapping, conflicting, forming thickets and tangles that thinned out into broad reaches of individuality and isolation. At the peak of the hill, they formed a great clot, and after that were gone forever.

"Can you see him?" The speaker, a mage of the Purple Order, could see nothing but an endless flow of faces—none of them heroic, none predestined to greatness. As far as he could tell.

"No," said the mage of the Green Order, who had been watching the septs as they crawled their way down history into oblivion, and was thoroughly bored. "Perhaps we should try a different construct."

"Or maybe he's not there at all," said Talu, the Purple mage. He had been bored for the last eight generations. He waved a hand, and the timeline faded away, leaving behind a view of blue skies and the soft, gentle roll of the hill.

"Well, he's somewhere!" said Kiso, the Green, with exasperation. "It stands to reason. He needs rescuing, so there must be a place he needs rescuing from." She felt logic was on her side in this, though she knew it was not infallible. "Sorry, Talu. I appreciate your help." She tried to make the apology sincere, but knew it came out grudgingly.

Talu shrugged. "What's an eternity between friends?" It seemed to him that he'd often spent eternities between friends, that an eternity spent in company was far preferable to one without. He found the concept difficult to put into words he could share. "Maybe he's just not in the septs, Kiso. What made you so certain he'd be there?"

Kiso shrugged in turn, grateful for a chance to move away from her short temper and her brittle edges, to put them, at least temporarily, in the past. "You know. Taunts of the Dark Lord. Posturing. Cryptic threats. Standard stuff."

"What exactly, though?" Threats varied, in Talu's experience. Some were more cryptic than others. Some were quite direct. There had been that time in his own universe, when a tyrant held a knife to his neck, and said, "Fill this basin with diamonds, or I'll cut your throat." Was it still a threat when there was no real risk?

"'I shall wipe his stain from the polished surface of my glory.' He's a real cleanliness freak, this Dark Lord." Though maybe it was more narcissism than asepsis. Dark Lords didn't usually focus on sanitation.

"They've all got something. But what makes you think that means here?" The threat was more vague than cryptic, in Talu's view.

"This is his glory." Kiso waved a hand at the hill where the septs had been. "The clans were violent, brutal, loved to fight, to conquer. Classic Dark Lord territory."

"And our hero came and put them right, did he?" Try as he might, Talu couldn't keep the sarcasm from his voice.

"Were you even listening at the Council?" Friends could be irritating, Kiso remembered now. It was best to keep some distance between them. "He didn't put them right. He was captured and tortured by the Dark Lord. Evil won out, and the world went to ruin."

"Oh. Vile Catstrophe #2, then." A little humor could sometimes straighten things out. Mages didn't seem to be good at making friends, but Talu was determined to try.

Kiso quirked a lip. Talu was careless, but he had a nice ironic perspective. She'd never been able to master it herself and her attempts always flew out as caustic barbs that fell like iron to the ground, avoided by one and all. "Right. So..."

"So we rescue him and Good triumphs again. Bully for us. If we can find him. Got it." It wasn't that Talu forgot these little details, exactly. They were just so... little. Defeating Evil, now that was a thing you could tell your father about. Not that Dad would ever ask how you did it. All he asked for was enough so he could say, "You done Good, son. You done Good." and then tell his buddies down at the Temple what a big man his little boy was.

It seemed to Kiso sometimes that Talu lived in a world of his own, metaphorically as well as literally. But he had come when she called, leaving behind his fogbound forests and rocky cliffs and their weird, slick creatures to come gallivanting through time and space with her. If that meant she had to handle the logistics, it seemed a small enough price.

"Listen," she said, though she thought he had been listening. "Maybe we're going at this the wrong way."

"Absolutely," he said. Kiso had mentioned she wanted a new construct. Thinking up new ways of visualizing the continuum; that was the fun part. Oh, sure, defeating the dark powers had its moments, but it was so... active, so frenetic. There was barely time to think up a clever spell sometimes, what with all the quarrels and gamma rays and prismatic sprays flying around. "What about this?" With a wave and a deft gesture, Talu conjured up the new construct he'd been considering. It was a draft, of course, a bit crude, but it had a nice subtlety to it, and it was nice to look at.

Kiso looked out at the grassy plain before them. As usual, with Talu, it was beautiful and inscrutable. "Very green," she offered.

He smiled. She'd understood! But he explained it anyway, just for the joy of pointing out the little touches. "The grasses are the populations, of course. See, those dense areas are the septs—how they expand and contract as they spread from past to future." He waved from right to left. "The darker the grass, the less tainted by evil. See how it gets dry and sparse over there? That's when most everyone has died, and those who remain are as foul as can be. Isn't it nice?"

It seemed counterintuitive to Kiso. Darker for better, lighter for darker? "And that's the Dark Lord, is it?" There was an elk munching her way across the field, pulling the grass up by the roots and swallowing it whole.

"Right! It should be male, of course, so the antlers can cast shadows of foreboding before it, but I haven't worked that part out yet."

"And the Dark Lord is male, of course," she pointed out. "Thus the 'Lord'."

"Whatever." Details again. Dad wouldn't be down by the altar talking about the gender of Evil.

"And this is helpful because?" It was nice to look at, Kiso admitted. Purple mages like Talu really had a handle on the stylistic aspects of magic, even if the technical underpinnings were sometimes weak.

"Well, your hero's going to be an aggravation, isn't he?" Of course he would; that was the point of heroes. "So all we have to do is watch the elk, see how he reacts. She."

Kiso nodded. It wasn't a bad plan, really. If only the elk weren't moving quite so slowly, and so clearly relishing her meal. A mouthful of souls here, a mouthful there, all so pleasantly bucolic that she almost forgot why they were there. "So, our hero will be like a wolf or something. Easy to see."

"It's spring, you see," Talu pointed out. You got the best, brightest colors then. Well, fall too, of course, but more in the leaves than in the grass, and he had all evergreens bordering the plain. And winter had some nice whites, but again, not really good for grass. And summer was dry. So, spring. Obvious when you really think about it.

"Very nice," she admitted. They should have brought a picnic. She wondered whether to have an imp go and fetch something, or whether Talu might think that an indication that she couldn't conjure up a good feast.

The elk twitched her neck, sending little fragments of grass flying to the side. She stopped her slow meander, tail flicking sharply as she reached her head back to nip at her flank.

"Hmm," said Talu. "I didn't plan for bugs." It was always the little touches that took time, the balance between elegance and verisimilitude.

The elk had moved on now, but they could see its skin rippling, and it walked with a hitch, as if something were crawling along its spine, an insect that she couldn't see or dislodge.

"I think..." Kiso said.

Talu sighed. "You may be right." It was so hard to judge the scale of things, really. The elk and the grass had seemed a nice touch. He hadn't thought it through, though. He could admit that now. The hero was a human, of course. They were always human. So, of course he would be tiny, even metaphorically. It was elegant, but not really poetic.

They watched as the elk, tormented by its gnat, or mosquito, or whatever the invisible pest was, twitched and bit and scratched with each hind leg, and at one point rolled over, flattening a wide swath of grassland. At last, one particularly nimble nip seemed to solve the problem, and the elk marched on, trampling the grass, but keeping its mouth firmly shut.

"That's it, then," said Talu. Not his best construct, but it had worked, and to a Green mage like Kiso, that was the key. All results and no presentation, that was a Green for you. But she was a nice one, and he was lonely. He wondered whether she'd like his tower room, with its view of the ocean, and the broad windows where you could hear the sea lions bark when you flung them open and let the fog in.

"That's it," Kiso agreed. And now the real work would begin. This artsy stuff was all very well, but it was the rescuing and defeating that was key. Leave it to a Purple, and the Dark Lord would conquer the world while the mage was figuring just the right flourish to cast a dissolution spell with. Talu wouldn't be much help here, but it wouldn't do to let him see that, and he could at least deal with the demons and monsters and so on. She wondered whether it would be too forward to invite him back to her little world after the battle. It wasn't much, just a cube of stone on a flat plain, but it was orderly, and it was home. Maybe he could help her decorate it a bit. Some flashes of color—mountains or clouds or suns or something. Whatever it was Purples did that made things seem cozy. Or maybe they could just go out. "Ready?" she asked, visualizing her spells as a neat row of ribboned boxes waiting to be opened.

"Ready," said Talu, manifesting a globe of coruscating power that would take them to the time and place where they now knew their hero was captive. "And listen. Maybe after... I know a little place with a great view of the firmament. Maybe we could spend a forever or two there?"

"Of course," she smiled as they dematerialized. "I'd love to."

B. Morris Allen is a biochemist turned activist turned lawyer turned foreign aid consultant, and now retired. He has lived on five continents, but the best place he's found is the Oregon coast. When he can, he makes his home there to work on his own speculative stories of love and disaster. He was the editor and publisher of Metaphorosis magazine for its nine year run.

Find out more at www.BMorrisAllen.com and on Bluesky @BMorrisAllen.com.

The Manor
by Stephanie Kvelſestad

Sunlight floods in through the cracked windshield.

You trace the crack with your eyes—they water. The sun is too bright. But you don't look away. If you finish tracing the crack before you drive past the upcoming tree, you will guarantee the visit will be a success.

One of your rituals. They change every day, but the practice is constant. Sometimes you hold your breath until the bus stops, other times you wait until the rabbit leaves before going outside. Everything is connected, everything has meaning. If you can only figure out what it is, you're golden.

The trip is a last-minute event. Last night, as you crawled into bed, turning on the television screen and muting the programming, you received a call from your mother. It was 10 after 11. Your mouth was dry, your hands shaking. You had been feeling anxious all day, what with the layoffs that would be ongoing throughout the week.

Nonetheless, you answer. If you can count past 5 before your mom says "Hello" everything will be fine.

"Hello?" you say into the phone. *1234567.*

"Hi, Sweety, I hope I didn't wake you," Patricia, your mother, says. Her voice is soft and sweet, always tired but so kind.

She didn't say 'hello', she said 'hi,' you think to yourself. What does that mean?

"Stacy?" she says.

"Yes, I mean no, you didn't. I was just about to go to sleep, but I'm still up."

"I'll cut to the chase, can you pick your grandma up tomorrow? I was supposed to go out and bring her back for the wedding..."

Your brother's wedding. It's the day after tomorrow. You have refrained from wearing socks all week to ensure the day will be a success.

"And I just found out there is a problem with the wedding venue and I need to drive out to the zoo with Sonia. Her mom is picking up her family from the airport and it would be a huge help if you could pick up your grandma."

A pause. She is waiting for my reply.

"Sure," I say before I can think too much about it. If she had asked me any earlier, I would have said no. It would have been too stressful.

"Life saver! I bet she'll even buy you lunch!" You can hear relief in your mother's voice.

You chat about the plans and then hang up the phone. The TV's flickering light covers you, protecting you as you drift to sleep.

*

Blurs of yellow and beige as fields of canola and wheat whip past the car. Here one minute, gone the next, yet continuing seemingly forever. The bright blue sky stretches like a canvas on which the clouds are painted. It is a beautiful day.

Cece, your grandmother, lives in Trochu. You've never driven there by yourself. For a long time, you didn't drive anywhere. Anxiety would flood your brain and you would have nightmares about crashing your car over and over again. Gradually, the nightmares began to fade as you started driving more and more, and made up rituals to keep yourself safe. Now, you can go just about anywhere.

The road is straight and narrow. Empty on all sides. Not even a bird in the sky.

You turn off the main highway just past the giant golf tee. Your grandma is waiting for you as you pull in front of her house. She is wearing bright white shoes, similar to the ones you have on. She is at the car door before you can exit the vehicle. Surprisingly quick for 88.

"Have you had lunch yet?" she asks, before saying hello.

1234567.

"Not yet," you reply. You can smell her perfume mixing with the scent of the fields and the bright sunshine. Warm flowers, soft hay, clear skies.

"I know a place," she says, hopping into your car.

You pull out of the driveway and follow her directions into town. It's a quiet day. Despite the beautiful weather, the streets are empty.

"A sad story. That house there, well one day smoke was just pouring out of it. Turns out Rad, the owner—nice guy but a bit too quiet if you know what I mean—died," your grandmother says as you drive past a boarded-up bright red house.

If you look in the upper window, you'll see a ghost. You shake your head. Nonsense. Nonetheless, you don't look.

"Oh!" Your grandmother throws her arm across you, pointing at the house across the street. "The lady in *that* house has gone to The Manor! Everyone is going to The Manor these days! Turn left at the corner."

"What's The Manor?" you ask, unsure if you should already know.

"Oh, there's Gwendolyn. Slow down," your grandmother says, rolling down her window.

"Gwenny!" She waves out the window. Gwenny glares at the car, squinting to see who it is. Her face transforms as she recognizes Cece. Suddenly she is years younger. A smile forms from ear to ear.

You stop the car in the middle of the road, anxiously looking in the rearview window. No one is behind you.

Gwenny hustles to the side of the car, grabbing onto the window frame for support.

"I got in!" Gwenny says. "I swear I must be the last person on the list, the town is practically a ghost—sorry Cece," Gwenny stops. Her cheeks flush. "And who is this?" Gwenny changes the subject and pokes her head in your direction.

"This is my granddaughter, Stacey. She's picking me up for the wedding tomorrow," Cece beams.

You sit up straighter in your seat and smile. "Nice to meet you."

"Oh good Lord," Cece covers her mouth with her hand. "Did you see that?"

You turn in your seat. A bright red van drives down the road, turning out of the residential area and towards the main highway.

Gwenny nods her head vigorously. "Go! Go! Go!" She hobbles away from the car, waiting for you to move. She leans on her cane with her forearm, keeping her hands free to clap.

"Stacey, turn the car around, we have to go home. I'm sorry but there might not be time for lunch after all," Cece says.

Curious, you drive back to your grandma's house. Your stomach lurches. You're not entirely sure why. If you see five birds before you get to your destination, it means you are hungry. If not... how much do you trust your intuition?

Waiting for the two of you on the front porch is a beautiful jewel-toned blue envelope. It is tied with a shimmering gold ribbon. You've never seen your grandmother move so fast. She flies out of the car, zooming to the front door. Like a starving lion, she tears into the flesh of the envelope, her hunger is unbearable for even a moment longer. She quickly reads the note before tucking it into her purse. Her mood visibly lowers. Composing herself, she makes her way back to the car.

"Is everything okay?" you ask. No birds in the sky.

"I've been invited to join The Manor," she replies. Her tone is matter-of-fact.

"That's great. Is it a club or something?"

Cece is lost in thought. Suddenly, she looks up at you. Her bright blue eyes are striking. You hold her gaze before looking away.

"Shall we?" You start to pull away from the house.

"Stop," Cece demands. Her eyes search for something she isn't finding. She is somewhere else. You recognize the face, it's one you make often.

Slumping in your seat, you remain quiet, unsure if you should turn the car off. You decide to text your mom. After pulling your phone from your pocket, you fire off a quick text.

Do you know what The Manor is?

The car door opens. Cece slips out silently. She is almost inside the house before you notice she is gone. Yep, surprisingly agile for 88.

"Grandma?"

Turning the car off, you follow her back towards the house. You reach for the door handle. It's locked.

"Grandma?"

You knock on the wooden front door, trying to see through the small stained glass window near the top. You can hear muffled conversation. Cece is talking to someone. No reply. She must be on the phone.

Creeeeeeek. The garage door creeks open. Cautiously, you make your way into the garage. The door to the house is unlocked.

"Grandma?" you say, stepping into the dark house. Your first instinct is to turn on the light. You resist, afraid of what you will feel if you flip the switch and the lights stay off. That is a bad omen.

"Grandma? Are you okay?" You ask. Your stomach turns, twisting inside of your rib cage.

"Almost everyone has gone to The Manor. It's the only place to go. I'm sure you understand," Cece's voice calls from down the hall.

Lingering in the doorway, you reach into your pocket and pull out your phone. Dialing your mom's number, you wait for her to pick up.

"Hi you've reached Maria, I can't come to the phone right now." It goes straight to voicemail.

"Help! Help! Jane, please, I'm hurt!" Cece calls from down the hall.

Your feet remain in place. Something is wrong. You feel pulled in two directions, frozen.

Across the entryway is a stool perched next to the front door. Slipping your phone into your pocket, you close your eyes. *1234567.* Silence. Walking up to the stool, you pick it up and hold it in front of yourself like a shield.

"Grandma?" you say, walking through the dark hall, once so familiar but today haunted by invisible shadows, blending into the dark. Like the shadows at the bottom of a pool, pretending to be sharks. Maybe you should turn on a light. *1234567. 1234567. 1234567.* You repeat this phrase in your mind like a mantra. A protective spell. You line up your steps with each group of 7, completing the ritual.

Stepping cautiously into Cece's bedroom, you reach for the light switch when you are hit in the back of the head by a blunt object. The surprise causes you to stumble over the stool. You cough as you land on your shoulder. Pain flares across your rotator cuff. You turn around just in time to see Cece hobble towards you from the ensuite bathroom, baseball bat in hand.

"Grandma!" you scream.

"Nothing personal!" Cece says before raising the bat once more above her head.

Horrified, you swiftly roll out of the way, crawling into the ensuite bathroom and locking the door behind you. Watching the door handle jiggle, you wonder if this is even real. Maybe you had an accident on the way to Trochu. You jump at the intense vibrations caused by Cece bringing the bat across the bathroom door over and over again.

"STOP IT!" you scream. This is not what you signed up for. Your grandmother is having a breakdown. It's time to call the professionals. Reaching for your phone, you panic. It's not in your pocket. It must have fallen out when you tripped.

You glance around the bathroom, listening to the symphony of your grandmother's screams and the banging of the bat on the wooden door. The bathroom window is too small for you to slip through. The only other way out of the room is through the bedroom. You're going to have to make a run for it.

Searching the bathroom for something to use to defend yourself, you pick up a can of spray deodorant and a towel, holding them in front of you like a sword and shield. Taking a deep breath in, you unlock the door and press your lips together. If you can get to the cordless in the kitchen before you take a breath, everything will be okay.

You step into the dark bedroom. It's too quiet. As you race out of the room, you scan the floor, searching for your phone. It's gone.

Your lungs begin to burn. You have to get moving. Stepping out of the bedroom, you scamper down the thin carpeted hall towards the kitchen. The cream-coloured cordless phone will be your salvation if only you can hold your breath until then. You consider running out of the house, but to what end? You would have to take a breath. What would happen if you failed to reach the phone before you took a breath? Surely nothing good. *1234567.*

Out of the darkness, a dense object soars past you, narrowly missing your head, slamming into the wall and dropping at your feet. You look down. It is a decorative rock, the kind your grandmother likes to put in her garden. *Love All,* the rock says in bright green lettering.

By now you are desperate to catch your breath. You feel your heartbeat across your body. You run to the kitchen, brushing the cordless with the tip of your index finger just before gasping for air. Phew. You made it. Safe for now.

Waaaaaaah eeh eeh eeh eeh. The dial tone is reassuring. It washes over you like a television screen's light. Good. Safe.

9-1-1 you dial into the phone, tucking yourself into the corner between the stove and the pantry.

Hsssss. The sound of a match strike is followed by the scent of smoke.

"Grandma?" you ask. Out of nowhere, a flaming walker burns toward you, sizzling with three Molotov cocktails tied onto it. The bottles are made out of cough medicine bottles. The fabric stripes are hand-knit.

Panicked, you grab the walker and pull it to the front door, throwing it onto the front yard just as it explodes, erupting like a volcano, and spreading fiery patches across the lawn.

"Hello 9-1-1. What is your emergency?"

"Hello, yes, I think my grandmother is having a breakdown. Do you know what The Manor is?"

You are halfway out the door, cordless phone in hand, talking to the operator when...

"Stacey? I'm scared..."

There is a frailty in Cece's voice. You linger in the doorway.

"Did you say The Manor?" the operator asks. The line goes dead. You dial again. 9-1-1. The phone rings and rings and rings. No one answers.

"Grandma? Are you okay? Do you have my phone? I think we need to get you some help," you say. The house is quiet. The kitchen is empty. Not so much as a dish in the sink. Just the lingering scent of burning yarn. *1234567.*

It is then that you see it. Your grandmother's purse. Hurrying, you open the vinyl flap and rummage around inside. There! The jewel-toned letter. You remove it from the bag and flip on the dining room light without thinking.

Under a golden *Confidential* written in fine calligraphy, the letter contains three simple instructions and an assignment.

Step 1: You must complete your initiation task.

Step 2: You must not tell anyone what your task is.

Step 3: You must provide proof that your task is complete.

Your task: We must enter The Manor without distractions. Your task is to kill what you love.

"Grandma! You can just kill the plants in your garden. What the hell!" You shout, shaking your head.

"I want a premium room!"

With that, Cece charges into the kitchen, as fast as an 88-year-old can. This time she does not have a baseball bat in hand, but an old rifle of her husband's.

"I put down two of my favourite dogs with this!" Cece says, lost in the memory for a moment. You use this fraction of a second to bolt out the front door. You move with instinct. No thoughts. No rituals. Just movement. Like a bird.

BAM! The rifle blasts a hole in the door just above your head as you run. Hands shaking, you unlock your car and floor the gas, ripping out of Trochu like a bullet out of a gun. The back window shatters as you turn out of the cul-de-sac and onto the main town road. Gwenny peers out of her windows at the scene. She shakes her head. "What a shame."

You drive home in silence, listening to the wind whistle through the broken back window. Your heart races. You don't think. For the first time in your life, you can't.

Tears begin to fall. A great release washes over you. The hot wet tears drip across your face. They are cold by the time they fall from your cheeks.

It's dark when you arrive home.

"Mom!" you shout as you run across the cool summer lawn.

"I've been trying to call you," a familiar voice says from the shadows. You see Sonia, one hand tucked behind her back.

"What? Where's my mom?"

"At work. A big project and she won't be home for hours. I need to talk to you," she says.

A chill travels down your spine.

"Where's my mom?" you ask, voice shaking.

"Have you heard about The Manor?" Sonia smiles cruelly, pulling out a butcher knife from behind her back. It glimmers from the shine of the stars.

"Everyone's going to The Manor," she says, elated. "Well, not everyone."

Sonia cackles as she throws the knife at you. The sound of her laughter fills the home like a sickness that will soon infect everyone.

*

You sit back on the couch. Your mom, dad, brother, future sister-in-law, sisters, future brother-in-law, grandma, and cousins look at you.

"What?" your brother says.

You shrug. "You asked me what could go wrong if I pick up Grandma Cece. So I told you."

Your family groans.

"She is never watching Olly," Sonia whispers to John, who nods his head.

"I was supposed to meet Nick twenty-five minutes ago." Lindsay looks at her watch.

"Haunted Paranormal was on tonight, Stacey. Haunted Paranormal." Your mom shakes her head, throwing her hands in the air.

"So who's picking up Grandma tomorrow?" your dad asks.

1234567.

Not it.

Stephanie Kvellestad is an HR Assistant with a passion for writing weird fiction. She has published four short stories. Currently, she is co-writing a found-footage horror film with her partner.

The Red Light
by J.M. Sanders

Before I saw the light, before the constant onslaught of red, before all of this, the thing that scared me most was the winding roads of rural Wisconsin. Not only do they twist through endless fields like some agricultural roller coaster, but America's Dairyland has the highest concentration of drunks. Point is, you can't just drift your way through a drive. Hands at ten & two, eyes peeled around every blind curve. It was one of these white-knuckle drives when I first saw the red light. It broke the pitch black of the woods like a supernova forming in deep space. It streamed from the window of a dilapidated house at least half a mile off the main road, looming on top of the hill.

I was still forty-five minutes away from Victoria, my on-again, off-again long-distance girlfriend—and five hours past my last cup of black coffee—when the red light snapped me awake, dropping my cigarette's burning cherry into my lap. Victoria and I had only been dating a few months, but things were going well. I'd met her online shortly after learning 2008 was a shit year to graduate, so I might as well take what I could get. Did I want to work in suburban Wisconsin? No. I wanted to be in Chicago, where the action was. But I go where the world takes me. And in 2008, it took me to Pewaukee, Wisconsin, a smudge away from the real 'Waukee in Wisconsin.

Victoria was never meant to be long-term. No offense to her—she just didn't fit with my lifestyle. I like to do what I want, when I want, without any commitment. But loneliness has a way of changing all that. Since I knew no one in Pauwakee besides my milquetoast coworkers, I did what any sensible lonely soul in the early 2000s did: online dating. When Victoria messaged me on Yahoo Personals of all places, I was cautiously optimistic. She was quirky. She was funny. She was sexy. And she wasn't looking to settle down anytime soon. The only problem was she lived all the way up in Madison. And while I didn't have a car, she did, even if it was a beater that could barely make the hour-plus drive.

Despite my distinct lack of commitment, we grew close. Close enough that we started seeing each other every weekend. We eventually got into this rhythm of swapping the car. She'd drive up for the weekend, leave the car with me, and take the train back. The following weekend, we'd swap again. And I loved those late-night drives. Just the road, music, and a cigarette. It was perfect. Until I saw the light. That fucking red light.

After snuffing the red-hot butt from burning another hole in my jeans, I slowed down. The amount of red pouring from this house, which would be right at home in a Tim Burton flick, was absurd. There weren't any other lights on in the house. Nothing on the porch. Nothing in the kitchen. Nothing for a good five-mile radius. Just one bright red light from the second floor's top bedroom. I took it for some angsty kid stuck in rural nowhere, reeling, listening to nu-metal in a bloodshot room. Like the burning ember on my lap, I brushed it off.

It was weird enough that I told Victoria about it that night. We were out back, enjoying one of my favorite views in all of Wisconsin: a field full of glowing fireflies. In the inky twilight of Victoria's backyard, on a lawn chair that could give you tetanus if you made the wrong move, you could see every constellation and every flickering firefly. That night, watching their tiny butts glow and fade, we were broken from our trance by a loud sizzle. Above us, another mosquito met its untimely end, zapping in a wave of electric tubes.

"Why do they do that?" Victoria asked, watching the scorched body fall away from the zapper, joining his dead buddies piled below.

"Think they're drawn to it. Like, they just can't resist."

"Yeah, well, they have brains the size of a pimple, so nuts to them."

I took a long pull from my beer, a delicious malty brew with a polka-dotted cow smiling back at me. I swallowed a slight buzz rising. "You ever see that red light off Route 59?"

She stopped mid-sip. "On the way to your place? If it's a red light, it's probably a whore house."

"No, it wasn't that. It was all alone. Nothing around for miles. Just trees, fields, and this two-story house. And a single red light on the second floor."

"You think a whore house would just be next to, like, a Walmart?"

I sighed. Victoria never took things too seriously. "It was just a bit... creepy, I guess. It was like it was trying to get attention. Inviting anyone brave enough to approach."

"Or horny enough." She downed her beer, giving me a look. "Speaking of..."

✳

I tried not to think about the red light for the rest of that trip. We went to farmers markets, eating squeaky cheese on long walks through the auburn fireworks of rural Wisconsin. We slept late, avoiding the morning chill creeping through our poorly insulated walls. We talked about getting a sourdough starter.

The weekend passed—as it often does when your entire relationship is concentrated to weekends—in a flash. Sunday afternoons had this bitterness to them. In some ways, I couldn't wait to be alone on my own again. But I couldn't deny that weekend me was better than weekday me. Better dressed, more motivated, even better looking. But to admit that meant I was feeling deeper things for Victoria. Long-term things. And my long-term plans did not involve any part of Wisconsin. I was a bird, and like Nelly Furtado, I had to fly away.

We drove to the train stop, both in our own melancholy worlds, lost in thought about the upcoming week without each other. We were a few miles away from the station when the stoplight ahead turned yellow. Instead of speeding through like I usually would, I slowed. I guess I just wanted a few more minutes with Victoria. The light changed from yellow to red.

I've seen stoplights my whole life and they're always a particular type of red. A three-year-old's fire truck. Primary school red. Friendly, yet authoritative. I know what stoplight red is, and today, hanging from the wire, the stoplight was not stoplight red. It was that red. That black as a moonlit night and all you can see is red, red. The exact shade of red I saw two days ago on the drive up, streaming from a rickety house.

I stared at that light, transfixed, unable to look away. Even as Victoria squeezed my hand, all I saw, all I heard was red. So obviously out of place in the comforting daylight. I felt it stare back, angry, speaking volumes with just 100 watts. A horn honked somewhere distant. Next to me, Victoria was talking but I couldn't make it out. All I saw, all I was, was red.

"Hello! Babe, the light is green." Victoria hit me on the arm. "Green means go, yo." I blinked as if waking from the tiniest of cat naps. Another horn honked behind us. I snapped out of it and slowly inched forward, the angry driver behind me skidding his tires. "What was that about?" She asked, looking at me like I was a squished bug.

I didn't know what to say. I barely understood what just happened, why I was so transfixed by that shade of red. Before I boarded the train, right as Victoria leaned in to kiss me goodbye, I couldn't help myself, "When you drive to my place next weekend, keep an eye out for that red light. The one in the two-story house off Route 59. OK?"

She rolled her eyes, grabbed my hat, and pulled it over my face, shoving me towards the train. "See you soon, lover boy."

*

It was a Wednesday when my boss brought me into her office, just off the central lab where I worked as an assistant to much more senior, boring scientists. "So, we've been doing some year-end planning, and your name came up. You've been here...?"

"Five months. Six in November."

"Right. Well, the team likes you. Your energy. Your attention to detail. There was talk about getting you a bit more involved. Maybe even lead a few projects?"

I paused. I liked it here, but leading a project meant staying on. Project leads were on for months, sometimes years. Being an assistant was simple. Help out where I was needed without being locked down to something permanent. And signing up meant...

There was a sudden glare. At first, I couldn't focus on it, but it came startlingly into view after a few blinks. The emergency light. The one you press when you get a chemical burn and need to start the shower. The emergency light should be off. But I saw red. That deep red I had forgotten about for a blessed two days.

"So what do you think?"

I stumbled back, knocking over a trash can, needing some air. I think I said thanks before I left. I walked purposefully, knocking over some glassware as my boss called out to me. Co-workers looked up from their workstations. I kept my head down. I tried to ignore them, ignore the light. But I knew it was shining for me.

I shook off Wednesday, knowing Friday was nearly here. Excited to see Victoria. Nervous to find out if she saw the light too. Daylight savings had just happened, so it should be dark, real dark. She'd see it. Still, she could get off early and pass by the house in the daylight. The light could have burnt out and been replaced by an energy-saving bulb. Or it was off for good, the power company finally cutting it for delinquent payments.

Eventually, way after the sun went down Friday night, I got a ding on my phone. Victoria was downstairs. I sprinted like a puppy, excited to see her after days apart. I jumped into her arms, but I could tell something was off. She held her keys in her hands, a slight tremble.

"What is it?" Asking, but knowing the answer.

She just shook her head.

"You saw it? The red light?"

She said nothing. I grabbed her tighter. Squeezing an answer out of her.

Her mouth tightened.

"Victoria?" She shook her head. I held her, trying to comfort. "It's OK. Tell me about the light."

Her face twisted. And then broke. She was laughing. Messing with me.

"I drove up 59 just like you asked. There wasn't any red light. Nothing." My face was blank. Not angry. If anything, a bit disappointed. Perhaps relieved. She stared at me, confused. "C'mon, I want to order Thai and forget about this week." She walked upstairs, beckoning me to follow.

That night, I couldn't sleep. I knew it was completely rational Victoria just missed the light. She was distracted when she crested over the hill. She wasn't really looking. Totally possible. But what kept me up was maybe she didn't miss the light at all—she was never meant to see it. It was my light to see. Only mine. I turned over, trying to sleep but failing. The room seemed bright, even with all the lights off. Every time I opened my eyes, I saw one thing. The standby light on my stereo. It was just a pinprick of red. A single LED assuring me power was on. But tonight, it seemed pretty red.

*

After a morning hike, we stopped by the store to pick up supplies for breakfast. We laughed, playfully pushing each other, grabbing sides of bacon, eggs, and cheese. Always cheese. Things seemed normal. Good. We even got supplies for our sourdough starter. The cashier started ringing us up, each item getting a friendly beep as it was scanned over the light. BEEP. The light got brighter. BEEP. Redder. BEEP. I stared. BEEP. I hated that light. BEEP. It was too much. BEEP. The light stinging my eyes. BEEP. I needed it to stop. BEEP.

I reached over the tiny barrier between us and the cashier, putting my hand over the scanner. "Please stop." The cashier stared back, confused. BEEP. I grabbed the cashier by the arm hard, too hard, my eyes never leaving the red glow emitting from the star-shaped scanner. "STOP. NOW."

"Can I help you, sir?" A man with a bushy mustache and a friendly name tag reading Manager Steve appeared.

Victoria, embarrassed, made up an excuse. "I'm so sorry." She threw down cash, abandoning the remainder of the groceries, including the container for our bread starter. "Can we just pay for what we have?"

Victoria yelled in the car on the way home. A lot. And she had every right to. I barely said more than "I'm sorry" and "You're right." After a while, the yelling stopped. She grabbed the groceries and started making breakfast. Angry breakfast.

Watching her smash eggs and viciously whisk batter, I couldn't help but smile. I snuck up behind, giving her a gentle hug. "Forgive me?" I asked.

Victoria looked back, scrunching her face the way she knew I liked. "You're still a big, stupid jerk, but…, Ok, don't be mad, but my parents have been asking about you, and I kinda, maybe, sorta told them I'd bring you over next weekend?"

On the stove, those tiny bubbles broke the surface of the pancake. I watched as the bacon popped in glorious grease. I watched as the stove light shined bright red. Saying hello again.

I didn't know what to say, so I nodded. I didn't do much for the rest of that trip. I know Victoria said things, important things about our future, but I couldn't focus. The red was back, and this time, not letting go. Victoria drove to the train station, leaving the car for me to drive back next weekend. It would never make it back to her. She got on the train, and I watched her until it was entirely out of sight. A sadness I couldn't define overwhelmed me.

I'd like to say I spent the week thinking about Victoria and our future. I'd like to say I thought about it for even a moment. But I couldn't. The red was here to stay. I saw it everywhere, every place, and it was time to see it again.

The following Friday, I left Pewaukee at 7:07 PM. I could have gone earlier—I didn't even bother showing up to work. Instead, I waited until darkness took over the sky. I stayed in Victoria's car. Hands at 10 and 2. Foot on the brake. Engine off. Basking in the glow of the brake lights. The red echoed off the garage walls, surrounding me. Basking everything in that red. My red. I sat in the car a full hour, soaking in that carnelian color like Vitamin D before I clicked over the engine. The red in the garage was swallowed up. I started driving out of town. I didn't need my GPS. I knew where I was going.

✱

Later, I couldn't tell you how much later, I crested over a small hill on a lone strip of road. I knew what was there. Like a sunset after a beach day, warm light bled through, cascading down the hill, covering the black with my special color. I drove higher, more red engulfing the car, shining for me. It was so bright. So wonderful.

I pulled over and put on my hazards, the red blinks matching the ruby hue spilling from the house. I got out, shut the door, and stared, content. The glow from the window illuminated a path to the front door, like a mission in a video game, right to my destination.

I took my first steps towards the house. And for the first time that drive, rational thought crept in. Turn around. Go see Victoria. Meet her parents. And for a moment, I wanted to. I wanted to keep driving. I wanted to make a good impression on Victoria's parents. I wanted that promotion. But it lasted only a moment. My eyes never left the light, my destiny.

I don't remember walking the path, but soon, I was at the front door, the red light right above me. So close now. I took one more look at the car, Victoria's car, those hazards bleating in rhythm, pulsing like a heartbeat. I reached out to the doorknob. The door was already open.

Inside, the house was silent, dried leaves from October's past crumpled up in corners, dead rotting things lumped together like yesterday's laundry. There was no furniture. Nothing but leaves and red.

I moved through the entryway into the living room, where the only piece of human existence was a key. It didn't look like a regular key. It was older, maybe for a hope chest or an attic. I picked it up, the dust around it leaving a perfectly clean imprint. I slid it into the tiny pocket of my jeans.

The kitchen was just as barren. Every shelf empty. Every drawer open as if raided in a hurry. There was one item left in the cupboard. A single can of tomatoes. The can was bulbous, rotten food attempting to burst through. Momentarily distracted, the red light called to me through the kitchen, reminding me of my final destination.

I went upstairs, light sweeping across me like a tractor beam. An alien ship welcoming me, gently pulling. I took another step. A wink of a smile on my face. Another step. More red.

My other senses blurred. I didn't hear the stairs creak—I didn't hear anything. My steps, my voice, nothing. I took a breath. The previous dankness replaced with emptiness. No sound. No smell. Nothing. Just red. Red covering the staircase. Red over an empty picture frame, haphazard on the wall. Red across my face as I reached the top of the stairs.

The room with the red light was in sight now. Angry scarlet flowed from the doorframe. I approached, never once feeling an ounce of fear. It felt right to reach for the doorknob. To grab that key from my tiny jeans pocket. To put it in and feel it twist without resistance. The door opened.

Soon, I'd understand. Understand why I saw the light and Victoria didn't. Why I came here. Why I stepped into this room. Why just this once, it felt so good to give in and go where I was told to go.

I stepped into the red room, puzzled. The light was there, a simple bulb hanging from a pull string. So red you couldn't see the wiring inside. As if full of blood, the light filtered through to produce a color like nothing else. This color echoed down the stairs, back down the path, to the car.

The car! I had a fleeting moment when my mind told me to leave immediately. But I'd come too far. This was my future now. Not with Victoria. Not at the lab. Right here.

Movement snapped me back to reality. Directly underneath the bulb—a figure cloaked in a tattered hoodie and filthy jeans sat comfortably. They gestured to me with a finger, thin, bony, with a nail so sharp and long, it could impale me right through my chest. The figure motioned to the only other object in the room—a single piece of chalk. They stood up, bones audibly snapping like a pinecone in a campfire. They invited me to sit. See. I slid forward, finding my footing. It was so bright. So red.

I sat. And I saw it all.

Illuminated on the walls, written neatly in orderly rows. The red light made the words clear as day, like a blacklight exposing hidden psychedelic messages. I stared at the names, hundreds starting at the top of the wall and falling to the bottom in neat columns. I scanned them, all of them crossed out. There were hundreds, maybe thousands. Each name written in different handwriting. Each name following the same orderly rows. Then I came to the last name on the list. The only one not scratched out with an ugly, angry line. My name.

I tensed, mentally cataloging everyone I'd wronged in the past. Why was my name on the wall? Did this figure know me? Was it randomly chosen? Was I just exceptionally unlucky? I took a beat, swallowing what felt like razor blades in my throat, barely able to finish my next thought.

What does it mean to have your name on this list? After all this time, I still don't know why my name was selected. But I knew what I must do next.

The figure moved to the wall of names at half speed. They pressed a piece of chalk, barely able to apply enough pressure, and crossed off my name. My body refused to move, frozen in place as if I'd been superglued to the floor. The cloaked figure inched towards me, eyes obscured by the dark hood. From inside, a mouth of rotten teeth smiled, not menacing, but at peace. They knelt down, knees popping like gunshots. They whispered right in my ear, smelling of burning hair and rotten flesh. They whispered a new name.

The cloaked figure crumpled, dust wafting across the red light in small, filthy modules. The door to the room shut, the lock engaged, and the light, my light, shut off.

Now it's my turn. To sit under this new shade of red. To wait patiently. To write the name whispered to me. I hope it's not yours.

J.M. Sanders started his writing career with his first story, "The Stinky King," in 3rd grade. Since then, he has worked for 15 years as a copywriter in advertising agencies, tech start-ups, and corporate behemoths. His writing has been published in Frazzled, Jane Austen's Wastebasket, Dark Harbor, and the once-popular, now-defunct Eat24 blog. He lives in San Francisco with his wife, son, and two possibly feral cats.

You can see more of his work at justinmsanders.com.

Garbage Day
by Tom Ramey

Doug had barely stepped inside his trailer when a sharp knock rattled the door. Someone must have been waiting for him; he hadn't even had time to kick off his work boots yet. His best guess was his cousin Terry trying to grab an after-work beer on the way home. Doug noticed an uptick in Terry showing up unannounced ever since his wife said no more alcohol in the house.

"Terry, you're going to have to start paying me for these beers." He said, opening the door.

It wasn't Terry. The man standing on his porch was the exact opposite of Doug in nearly every way. A high and tight fade instead of Doug's shaggy mane, shiny dress shoes instead of battered work boots, and most of all a suit instead of blue jeans and flannel.

Doug didn't think he even knew anyone who wore suits other than the church folk, and they stopped knocking on doors to save souls years ago. The man looked like he could be Doug's father, but they were probably the same age.

"Are you Mr. Aldean?" the man asked.

Doug crossed his arms. "Maybe. Who's asking?"

Doug knew it was a petty rebellion, but something about this guy screamed authority, and Doug never liked being told what to do.

"I'm Thomas Carrigan with the National Security Agency." He produced a badge from his inner jacket pocket, then tucked it away before Doug could get a good look. "I'd like to ask you a few questions, if that's okay."

Doug had never been in trouble with the law, other than some underage drinking incidents, but he watched a lot of television.

"I'd like a lawyer, please."

Carrigan furrowed his brow. "Why?"

"I don't know. They always say you shouldn't talk to the cops without a lawyer, and you're supposed to provide one for me."

"Mr. Aldean, I'm not here because I suspect you've committed a crime. In fact, if you have committed a crime of some sort, I don't want to hear about it. I just have some questions about last Thursday, around seven in the morning."

Doug hesitated, then shrugged. "Alright, I guess. Come on in."

Doug gestured for Carrigan to sit on the couch, while he sat in a recliner.

If Carrigan noticed the number of empty beer cans on the coffee table between them, he didn't show it. He flipped open a notebook. "I have a report that you were seen chasing a raccoon out of your yard that morning."

Doug blinked. "What? No. I didn't chase a raccoon anywhere. Aren't they nocturnal? Wouldn't even be running around that time of day."

Carrigan scribbled something down. "Perhaps it wasn't a raccoon. A possum, maybe?"

Doug gave him a look. "Aren't those nocturnal too?"

Carrigan exhaled sharply, then adjusted his approach. "Alright. A small animal was seen running across the street, and you were seen running after it. Ringing any bells?

Doug scratched the back of his head. "Oh! Juniper."

"Juniper?"

"Yeah. That fat cat Juniper. Belongs to an old lady a couple houses down." Doug shifted his weight in the recliner. "I wasn't chasing her. She was napping near the dumpster, and when I tossed my recycling, it scared her awake. She ran like a bat outta hell."

Carrigan perked up. "We're making progress. I guess my next question is, why did you throw your recycling out?"

Doug stared at him. "What do you mean, why?"

"Did you do it by accident?"

Doug snorted. "How the hell do you throw out recycling by accident?"

Carrigan remained unfazed. "Did someone else tell you to take it out?"

"No."

Carrigan's eyes started to glisten. "Okay, so why did you throw it out, at that time, on that day?"

"Thursday is recycling day, and I leave for work around seven. Why do you care about my recycling so much?"

Carrigan's eyes lit up. "So, you took out your recycling completely of your own free will?"

Doug threw up his hands. "Yes!"

Carrigan grinned. "This is fantastic."

"What the hell is going on?"

"Well, the cat you scared ran into the street causing a minor car accident."

"Hey, I can't be liable for that!"

Carrigan shook his head.

"No. I mean, probably not. I wouldn't be here about something like that."

He paused to gather his thoughts.

Carrigan snapped his notebook shut. "Mr. Aldean, you may have stopped World War Three."

Doug was starting to think the badge he saw earlier was fake. He gestured vaguely toward the door. "Right. Well, you're welcome. Glad I could help."

"Wait! I know how this sounds." Carrigan leaned forward. "Last Thursday, there was a political fundraiser in the city a few miles from here. It was brunch with the President and a few foreign dignitaries. One of those thousand-dollars-a-plate affairs. An assassination attempt was thwarted there. I've spent all week tracing back what led to the assassin getting caught."

Doug crossed his arms. "And my garbage is part of that?"

"Yes." Carrigan's excitement was building. "The most important part, the catalyst to a chain of unlikely events. Here's how it happened. Officially, a Secret Service agent noticed something off about the assassin, tried to detain him, and in the struggle, the guy was knocked unconscious. What really happened is the agent slipped, bumped into the guy, and he fell down some stairs. That's when they found his gun."

Doug raised an eyebrow. "How'd he get a gun in there?"

Carrigan waved the question away. "He 3D-printed it. Single-use plastic. No metal detectors picked it up."

Doug whistled low. "Alright. What does this have to do with me?"

Carrigan leaned in. "The President said he refused to believe we simply got this lucky. Someone made a conscious decision that led to this happening. That person saved the world. Find them.'"

"How does some guy slipping twenty miles away have anything to do with me taking out my recycling bin?"

"The reason the agent slipped was because a waiter had dropped a glass from a table they cleared at the brunch. When I talked to the waiter it was clear they were hungover from the night before. Turns out they weren't even supposed to work that day. They were woken up by a phone call from the catering company asking them to come in because the waiter scheduled had gotten into a car accident."

"You can't be serious."

"Yes." Carrigan nodded. "The car accident? It happened right here, in front of your house. The driver swerved because something ran away from you, into the road."

Doug pressed his fingers against his temples. "So, you're telling me... I take out my recycling, which scares a cat, which runs into the road, which causes a car accident, which makes a hungover guy go to work on his day off, which makes him drop a glass of water, which makes a Secret Service agent slip, which takes down an assassin." He looked up. "That what you're saying?"

Carrigan smiled. "It was orange juice, but yes."

Doug exhaled. "Okay. I don't really know what to do with this information, but uh... you're welcome for saving the world, I guess."

Carrigan reached into his jacket and pulled out a small, lacquered box. "We can't do the normal ceremony due to the optics of the situation, but the President wanted to make sure whoever started the chain of events received this."

Doug flipped open the box and stared at the medal inside. It was a fancy-looking thing. It had a five-pointed white star trimmed in gold, with a blue circle in the center where a tiny golden eagle spread its wings like it owned the place.

The whole thing hung from a thick blue ribbon with white edges—the kind of thing you'd expect to see draped around a war hero's neck, not sitting in the grimy hands of a guy who barely remembered to take out his recycling half the time.

It had weight to it, both in his palm and in the absurdity of the moment. Doug turned it over, half-expecting a joke engraved on the back, but no, it was real. Official. Probably worth more than his trailer.

"That's the Presidential Medal of Freedom. It's the highest award a civilian can receive in the United States. No one will ever know about this, but thank you for your service to your country."

After he left, Doug opened a beer and sat in his kitchen.

"I guess recycling really is good for the planet."

Tom Ramey is a horror and crime fiction writer that has been a fan of works in the genre since long before he should have been allowed to consume them. He's recently been published by Close to the Bone Publishing, Suddenly and Without Warning, and Flash Phantoms. Currently living in Delaware with his wife and three kids, he is querying is first novel.

Three Trash Nights
by Julius Fish

John craved male interaction. His wife, four daughters, and two female dogs left him stranded on a testosterone island in a sea of estrogen.

He loved his family and couldn't have been prouder to be a father of four girls, but with his career as a stockbroker and raising his children, John fell out of touch with his friends. As a man, every now and then he needed to talk to another man. There was no talking to his co-workers because they were a bunch of disgusting pigs.

That didn't mean he felt unhappy with his life. It simply meant John needed some good ol' fashioned male bonding. Nothing wrong with it. Which was why his favorite part of every week became Tuesday night.

Tuesday nights were trash nights in his neighborhood. Everybody dragged their blue, city-issued, plastic garbage bins down the driveways and placed them by the curb. Through this, John developed a friendship with his neighbor, Evan.

Evan was a writer who didn't get out much. He lived alone. Other than a random woman here and there, nobody went in and out of his house. John imagined him sitting in his study with a big oak desk wandering through far-off lands; having a blast as he put down words describing the images, sounds, and smells in his head. John often thought how exciting it must be to be creative for a living.

Every Tuesday night, John sat by his window and waited for Evan to take out the trash.

*

The first trash night came.

Lights above Evan's garage flashed when it opened. John sprinted to the door. Blood pounded in his ears as if his heart were a ticking bomb seconds before explosion. His time had come.

He stepped into the cool fall air. A waning moon provided little light to drown the glinting stars above. It reminded John of camping trips as a child. Lying on his back in the forest, staring at stars past stark silhouettes of evergreens.

The weather was perfect on this trash night. Not cold enough to require a jacket; not hot enough to make John sweat; not any temperature but the right one. Dead leaves on the cement crunched under his feet, releasing pleasant autumn odors.

Dueling sounds of plastic on pavement permeated the not-so-humble suburban neighborhood as both John and Evan dragged their garbage bins to the bottom of their driveways.

They faced each other. An orange streetlight between the two cast long shadows on their lawns. John nearly passed out from excitement. It's the little things.

"How's it going?" John asked, wondering if he sounded too desperate?

Evan set his garbage bin and gave a friendly smile. "Good, and yourself?"

"Oh, you know, I don't dream at night because I'm living it."

John waited for Evan to laugh, and as soon as he chuckled, John joined in. John was quite proud of the joke. He spent most of last week coming up with it.

"That's a good one," Evan said. John fought the urge to faint. "Do anything interesting over the weekend?"

"With the warm weather on Saturday, I took the wife and girls out on the pontoon. Although when they aren't around, I like to call it the *poontoon*. Just a little guy humor." They exchanged another laugh. "I would never cheat on Sandra, don't worry. How about you?"

"I was in Los Angeles through the end of last week and over the weekend. They want to adapt one of my books into a movie."

How exciting! John thought.

"How exciting!" John said.

Evan's lips pursed into a tight line. His blue eyes—shining but a moment ago—dulled. "Yeah, exciting... How are the wife and kids?"

"Good, good." How could a single man with such an amazing career care about a life as boring as John's? "My oldest found—"

"Camille?"

"That's right, Camille. Camille found out yesterday she got the lead part in her school's play, so we're all over the moon for her." John looked at the sky. Evan followed his lead. "Or should I say, we're all over the *waning crescent* for her."

Up and down the street bounced booming laughter. Full of zingers that night, John was.

"Very exciting," Evan said.

This man, who wrote such elegant and beautiful stories, revered by readers and critics alike, thought John's life was exciting. Wow.

They stood in silence a few moments longer.

"Well," Evan said. "I better get going. Take care of yourself, John."

"You too."

Both men went their separate ways. John closed the front door behind him and slid to the ground, skin tingling. What a rush. What a thrill, he thought. Man, that was another good trash night.

John's wife Sandra stopped in front of him. "How's your boyfriend?"

"He's not my boyfriend."

A big, toothy grin cracked her face. "Whatever you say." She giggled to herself and continued on her way.

The next trash night came.

John did as he always did and waited by his front window. Once Evan's garage lights flashed, John bolted to the door.

Colder tonight than it was last week. He grabbed a light jacket and threw it on. He pulled his trash can across the concrete and looked up. No moon tonight, but stars still stood against the clear black sky.

John met Evan under the orange streetlight. He kept his hands in his pockets so Evan couldn't see him flexing his fingers excitedly.

"How's it going?" John asked, thinking he sounded too desperate. Idiot. Big dumb fool.

Evan's clouded eyes didn't meet John's but instead remained fixed on something unseen. Far off in the distance as if an invisible monster waited for his moment to lay waste to all the not-so-modest homes of the not-so-humble suburban neighborhood.

"Fine.," Evan said. "And yourself?"

"Oh, you know. I don't dream at night because—"

"Because you're living it," Evan interrupted. "You said that last week."

John's cheeks burned with the white-hot intensity of an exploding sun. How could he be so stupid?

Evan smirked. "It's still funny though. I like it."

Cold autumn air kissed John's face, and his cheeks cooled. "Do anything interesting over the weekend?"

Evan shook his head. His eyes remained looking at the invisible monster. "No. I had some calls with the screenwriter adapting my book." His lips turned into a scowl. "Nothing interesting."

John, never a man good with words, often found himself at a loss for them. This was one of those times.

After a period of silence, Evan said, "What about you? How's… um…" he squeezed his eyes shut and scratched his head.

"Camille?" John suggested while wondering what he did to ruin this incredible friendship.

"That's right. Camille. How's her play coming along?"

"It's still in the early stages. They started doing table reads this week, but I think she loves it. I've never seen her talk so passionately about something before." For the first time that night, Evan's eyes met John's. "She's in sixth grade so it will probably change a hundred times over the next year, but I think she really wants to be an actor."

John came out here to get away from his wife and daughters, but here he was talking about them. Not only talking about them, but pride rose within in him as every word left his mouth. This was supposed to be his guys' night, and he was destroying it.

"She wants to be a professional actor?" Evan asked.

"Yes."

"Hollywood?"

"No," John said. "I have the one child on Earth who prefers reading to keeping her eyes glued to a screen. She wants to be on Broadway."

For the first time that night, Evan smiled. "Smart girl."

They stood in silence once again.

"Well," Evan said. "You take care of yourself, John."

"You too."

Both men went their separate ways. John closed the front door behind him and stared at his feet.

So many jokes and clever things to say, but none of them came out. Instead, John talked about Camille. He constantly had discussions centered around his children with Sandra, teachers, and every other parent he knew. His daughters absorbed most of his life, and there was only one night a week to take a break.

Why not leave Camille be? Why not consider something else? Why not talk about something masculine? Like chopping wood. Neither one of them chopped wood, but they could've shared their opinions on it. John didn't move and glowered at the hardwood.

Sandra stopped in front of him. "Did Evan let you get to third base tonight? Or does he want you to meet his parents first, so he knows things are serious?"

"That's not funny," John said.

"It's a little funny." Sandra giggled to herself and continued on her way.

*

The last trash night came.

Light's above Evan's garage flashed, and John ran to the door. An unseasonably cold night. John wore a scarf, wool-knit cap, and winter jacket. Clouds blanketed the sky. Dark with no stars or moon. Stiff winds tossed his scarf about his neck as he hauled the garbage bin toward the orange glow of the streetlight.

Evan stood shirtless—staring. John searched for what he glared at, but found nothing.

He must be freezing, John thought.

But Evan showed no signs of discomfort. His feet planted firmly on the ground. His shoulders square, facing the not-so-dark shadows cast from the not-so-humble homes of the not-so-modest suburban neighborhood. Silver trails of smoke left a burning cigarette.

"How's it going?" John asked.

Evan didn't move. After a few seconds, he breathed deep and let out a long breath. "Autumn is the season of the dying. Followed by winter, the season of the dead."

John spun around. Whipping his arms in every direction like one of those inflatable things shady used-car dealers put everywhere during their year-end clearance sale.

"What?"

Evan put the filter end of the cigarette in one nostril. He used his thumb to close the other and inhaled. Embers glowed brighter as the cigarette shrank half an inch. Two long streams of smoke flowed from his nose as he exhaled.

"Are—are you smoking through your nose?" John asked.

"I don't like the way cigarettes burn my throat," Evan said. "I drag through the nose because by the time it hits the back of my throat the smoke cools off."

"Doesn't that burn your nose?"

"I prefer a burnt nostril to a burnt throat."

John contemplated deeply for a moment before saying, "Okay. So... How're you doing, Evan?"

Evan took another drag through his nostril and flicked the butt into the street. He stomped to John's driveway and seized him by the lapels, pulling their faces close together. Eyebrows furrowed so intensely that a crevasse on his forehead resembled the Grand Canyon.

"How does it look like I'm doing?"

Evan breathed harsh smoke into John's face with a tone just as harsh.

John fought the urge to cough. He tried to break free from the involuntary embrace and put some distance between them, but Evan's hands might as well have been a vice grip.

With a look of terror John said to him, "Not well."

"You're damn right not well!" Evan's words echoed off the asphalt. "Those MBA bastards at the movie studio want to change the main character of my story from a woman to a man. They are completely disregarding the themes and essence of the character because—and I quote—" Evan made air quotes while impressively maintaining the grip on John's coat with his other fingers. "'—It will play better with the demographics of the genre according to the marketing department.' It's terrible!"

"That *is* terrible," John said.

"You're damn right it's terrible!"

As a stockbroker, John knew little of the creative life. Why it was so terrible, he didn't understand. But judging from his current predicament, it clearly had an impact on Evan.

Bottom lip trembling, John rifled through his brain for the right words. "It's just the movie. You still have the book. People loved the book. I loved the—"

Crack! Evan slapped John. Like a lead ball firing from a cannon; John's hat rocketed off his head. Blinding pain erupted from his face.

"You don't get it!" Evan yelled.

"I guess I don't" John said, holding back tears.

"You're damn right you don't!" Evan released John and shoved him to the ground. "Your wife is pretty and witty. Your children are all charming and kind. Your job is boring and quite stable."

The boring part was a tad unnecessary, John thought.

"I have nothing! Nothing other than my work. Nothing. If you died today, five wonderful women in that house will mourn you. If I died today, some fans will be disappointed they won't get another story out of me to occupy their lives for a few weeks. And a handful of critics may say, 'It's a shame he's dead, but his writing always was a bit derivative. It had a tendency to insist upon itself.' What does that even mean? *It insists upon itself?*"

John hadn't the slightest idea. He pushed himself to his feet. Several things ran through his mind as to what to tell Evan, but he knew his friend—former friend—was a lost ship. John's father got lost years ago, and those memories came rushing back to him. He gulped down a lump in his throat.

When people went crazy like this, saying anything logical only exacerbated the problem. They must find their own way back to shore. If they needed any help navigating, they had to ask for it, and even then, there was nothing more a person could do other than show them the way.

Evan sighed and lit another cigarette through his nose. "I'm sorry I hit you."

"It's fine," John said, rubbing his face where the hand struck. It wasn't fine.

"I get so worked up over my art. I pour my heart and soul into every story and every character. They reflect me.

"It's frustrating with studios changing things around to accommodate the audience. Great art is not bending. Not bowing. Great art is an expression of one's soul for the world to breathe in and interpret."

Evan's posture shifted. Matching a politician addressing a crowd. "My name is Ozymandias, king of kings; look on my works, ye Mighty, and despair!"

Evan snickered and took another drag. Still through his nostril.

Not a single word escaped John's lips. All he wanted was to spend time with a normal guy once a week. Was that too much to ask for?

"I suppose I should remember how that poem ends," Evan said. His voice now gravelly and grating. "Everything will come to an end and be forgotten eventually. No art—no matter how great—can escape the sands of time. You, me, your wife, your children, every man, every woman, everyone else, somewhere in between man and woman will one day die. Any trace of our existence shan't remain."

The world slipped from beneath John's feet. Falling, the singular sensation. Into a bottomless pit, John was falling. Falling and flailing. Flailing and hoping. Hoping and wishing. Wishing he might once again reach solid ground, but it never came. Tears streamed from John's eyes.

"I better get going," he said and rushed back to the house.

Evan turned and looked back at the street. "Take care of yourself, John."

John said nothing. He hurried inside and slid down the front door. He rubbed a hand over the smooth hardwood.

Why can't anyone be normal? John thought. He wanted to talk about football, golf, and chopping wood—even though he didn't chop wood. Was that too much to ask for?

John sobbed. Salty tears hit the floor with a pit-pat. Gobs of snot shot from his nose.

Sandra stopped in front of him. "So, did he let you see his —are you crying?"

"Girls!" John yelled. "Girls, come down here for a second!"

One by one, John's daughters filtered in from different parts of the house. Their two female dogs came as well. The women of his life observed him with concern.

"Come here," John said and motioned them toward him. "Come here."

They crouched to the ground. He wrapped his arms around them. The falling stopped. On solid ground, John landed.

"Are you okay, Dad?" Camille asked.

"I'm much better now," John said. "I love you all so much. Never forget how much I love you."

Julius is a writer located in Cleveland, Ohio. He loves three things in this world more than anything else, his wife, his dog, and writing, in that order. Although, his wife argues the dog comes first.

Barry Must Be Stopped
by Alyssa Beatty

Excerpt from a diary found in the wreckage:

April 6th

Barry must be stopped. No matter the cost.

*

Carol woke with a start, heart pounding.

"Not again," she whispered. She pulled on her favorite fuzzy pink bathrobe.

The sound that had ripped her from sleep, akin to the dying lament of a tone-deaf swan, grew louder as she approached the garage door.

"Are you going to be much longer?"

Barry's turtle-like appearance was intensified by the drum strapped to his back and the way he squinted at her from beneath the cymbal atop his head. The accordion on his chest wheezed mournfully. The trumpet hanging from a cord around his neck glinted in the harsh overhead light.

"I gotta practice, babe."

"It's three a.m."

"Muse strikes when she strikes."

"Okay."

Carol drifted down the hallway and opened the closet door.

The box on the floor was still sealed. She'd been hesitant to use the device; all the online reviews were positive, but she was always skeptical of those.

The accordion wailed, punctuated by the arrhythmic, sugar-crazed-toddler-banging-on-a-pot thump of a bass drum.

Carol opened the box. The hourglass—filled with sand that glinted an odd silver—fit neatly in the palm of her hand.

A trumpet squonked like an enraged Canada goose.

Carol closed her eyes. "Take me back. Back to that terrible day."

She turned the hourglass over and vanished in a flash of light. A scrap of paper floated to the hallway floor. *Warning* (it said): ***More than ten (or possibly twelve) uses of this product will lead to timeline warpage and the extinction of life on earth. Even the cute stuff, like capybaras.***

April 6th

Six failed attempts to dissuade Barry from buying the infernal contraption. I've tried pleading, reasoning, and bribery; he just keeps asking why I want to stifle his joy. I need to alter my tactics.

Note to self: leave a positive review of Pickpocketing for Dummies online. So helpful!

Barry stood in front of a window display, grinning at The Fantabulous One-Man-Band Set.

"Look at that! It's amazing. Don't you think? Babe? What are you doing in my pocket? Feeling frisky? Oh, my wallet. Thanks, I was looking for that."

April 6th. Again.

Five times I've tried and failed to lift Barry's wallet. He's just too alert. Considering putting Nyquil in his coffee to slow his reflexes but torn on whether red or green would be the less noticeable flavor. Also considering downgrading my review of Pickpocketing for Dummies to three and a half stars.

The hourglass is making an irritating sound. I don't know what it means. They really should have included instructions.

✳

Carol looked hopefully at Barry over the edge of her coffee cup.

He took a sip and grimaced. "This coffee tastes like... green."

"Dammit."

Barry poured his coffee into the sink. "Let's go for a walk. Do some window shopping. What's that noise?"

Carol sighed and pulled the beeping hourglass from her bathrobe pocket.

✳

April 6th. AGAIN.

Despite dying eight years ago, Barry's mother called this morning. OF COURSE she's on his side about the one-man-band.

I wish the hourglass had come with a warning about potential side effects, like mothers-in-law coming back from the dead. At least it finally stopped that annoying beeping. And having Sylvia in our lives again is a small price to pay if I can keep Barry from ever seeing that thing. I just have to try harder. Maybe it's time for more direct action.

Carol lurked beneath a streetlight. She glanced furtively up and down the deserted street and pulled a rag-stuffed bottle and a lighter from the pink depths of her bathrobe.

*

April 6th. Has it ever been any other day?

Note to self: attempted destruction of the music store leads to immediate arrest. Luckily, I escaped before being booked. I've heard fingerprint powder is impossible to get out of terrycloth.

Considering leaving a negative review for the hourglass. They really should have warned about side effects, e.g., the sky turning orange and the sudden appearance of the new neighbors, of whom I am NOT A FAN.

*

Carol looked down at the jumbled mass of the Fantabulous One-Man-Band Set and hoisted a sledgehammer over her shoulder with a grunt.

Barry frowned at her from the doorway. "What are you doing?"

"Please, Barry. If you care about me at all, let me do this."

"Of course I care. But that's my passion. Do you really want to smash my passion?"

"Yes?"

"Babe. No, you don't. You'd never stifle my joy like that."

Arvin, the Ankylosaurus from across the cul-de-sac, stopped at the end of their driveway.

"Hey, Barry. You playing tonight? Me and the boys might come listen again."

"Absolutely. More the merrier."

"Cool." Arvin shuffled away.

"Stay off the lawn this time, Arvin!" Carol called after him. "Your tail tears up the grass."

"Calm your tits, Carol," Arvin called back.

"Go extinct!"

"Babe. That's, like, super offensive in their culture."

Carol growled and reached into her pocket.

April 6th. Always. Forever.

Well, now we have meteors. Arvin's running around yelling, "Not again!" I'd feel bad for him if my yard wasn't such a mess.

Barry plays day and night. He says it's important to boost morale, and people do come in droves to listen. I tell them to go home, that the meteors raining fire and the rude dinosaurs and Sylvia living in our basement are ALL HIS FAULT. But they can't hear me over the cacophony.

Note to self: upgrade review of Pickpocketing for Dummies back to five stars. I make a decent living off the crowds, which is good, because my office is now a primordial swamp.

Tried to leave a negative review for the hourglass re: lack of warning over annoying side effects, but apparently the company never existed.

Carol's fuzzy pink bathrobe was an errant pop of color against the smoking ruin of the cul-de-sac. Behind her, in the wreckage that had been their garage, the whine of an accordion, the thump of a bass drum. A cymbal crashed, a trumpet squealed. She pulled the hourglass out of her pocket.

He must be stopped. No matter the cost.

Alyssa Beatty lives in Brooklyn, NY. When she is not unsuccessfully trying to keep her cats off the kitchen counter, she writes short speculative fiction. Her work has appeared in Penumbric Speculative Fiction, Luna Station Quarterly, and Spread: Tales of Deadly Flora.

Good Company
by Torrey Francis Malek

"We have company coming," she warned.
I immediately noted the royal we.
By instinct, I glanced at her face—
Cold as porcelain dinner plates, her lips
Without a hint of a mischievous curl.

"When?" I thought, "What day, and hour?"
"Today," she said, dour, "tonight."
Too late to fortify the ramparts,
Or strip naked and wander away
Into the loblolly pines and their shadows.

Woe be mine, like Momus's own plight.
If there were wheels, I'd tow this house far
From all callers. Were there oars, I'd row
Till the only eyes pried were clams
Laid open wide for a fine chowder.

But here I stand, a trembling host,
Polishing silver never meant to be admired,
Airing curtains of dusty ghost throats
whispering of visits before and nevermore,
The doorbell knelling solitude's end.

I check the weather apps again, hoping
Regrettably clear skies, no tornadoes to save me.

Maybe I'll toss a word between foes
And watch them lunge like jesters
Before the King's indifferent court.

Too late for defenses or trenches now,
While she wraps piglets in blankets below,
I retreat up the attic ladder, armed
With some paperback Whitman for a wit's end,
A loaded bottle of scotch and some absconded prosciutto.

Yet, in the laughter that fills the hall,
A strange, unexpected joy takes shape,
Finding myself tallying smiles like poker chips,
Pouring drinks like the bartender owes me a favor,
Realizing somewhere between the cheese plate
And the third awkward hug at the door
That perhaps the secret to hosting is this:
To dread it all, resist the urge to flee,
And then discover, with some absurd delight,
How oddly comforting it is
To play the part of the unwilling host,
Only to find you've been waiting for guests all along.

Torrey Francis Malek is a poet and essayist whose work moves between two distinct literary modes: one of deep personal reflection and nature-inspired lyricism, and another of humor and sharp-edged satire. His poetry has appeared in the Broadkill Review and he is a frequent contributor to the Plants & Poetry Journal. In 2023, his work was recognized on the Shortlist for the Letter Review Prize for Poetry.

A Witch Out of Water
by Melanie Mulrooney

Emily Fairweather enjoyed a solitary life in her little tea shop in the woods. She spent her days creating herbal medicines, poring over a vast collection of leather-bound books, and tending to an occasional visitor in need of magical services.

One early fall day, she was out sweeping the front step—the oak tree had taken to throwing acorns at her cottage after a recent pruning—when she tripped over a package that hadn't been there a moment before. She unwrapped the brown paper to find a travel directive in the form of a small oil painting. While she would have preferred to disregard the missive, she was a seventh-generation witch with the Order of Panacea, pledged to maintain magical order. Ignoring her duty was as impossible as explaining the need for a trim to an irate oak tree.

She allowed herself just five minutes of irritation—it was hard to resist the latest Cruella Smythe novel calling from the table beside her favourite green armchair—before shifting attention to the bright side of the situation. As much as she hated to leave home, it did get a little lonely in her tea shop, given the infrequent visitors. An opportunity to meet new friends might be just what she needed.

A large green travel satchel sat near the door, ready for Emily's next adventure. She added items that might be needed for the trip: herbs and remedies for injuries, standard tools for magical assistance, and a couple changes of undergarments. Last in was a flask of her strongest elderberry wine, in case she was the one in need of fortification.

Emily slung the bag over her shoulder and picked up the oil painting depicting her destination. The meadow of wildflowers was vibrant and textured, rendered in a riot of colours from the palest green to the deepest red. She ran her fingers over the river, which was depicted with such realism it was a shock to find it dry to the touch. She could smell the bergamot and anise hyssop, feel the brush of delicate yarrow leaves, and hear the water flowing over rocks. It was all very soothing, sparking hope that perhaps this trip wouldn't be so bad after all.

Reaching into her bag, Emily grabbed a pinch of gold travel dust and sprinkled fine flakes onto the painting—adding an intention to be standing in the meadow. A flutter started in her belly and she closed her eyes to avoid the worst of the vertigo that always accompanied these trips. Her body felt weightless—that part was quite enjoyable—as the disorientation of nothingness swept through her. Then, within a moment that seemed to last forever, she felt her feet land on solid ground.

Emily opened her eyes, anticipating a pretty view. Instead, she was greeted by something wet and slimy, which turned out to be a large trout, slapping her in the face.

She landed in the middle of a battle between two young women. One was standing in the river, water to her knees. Her long hair flowed into the stream, forming an effective net around her body. The other—red-faced and feral—stood on the bank, gripping a wooden paddle, a pail full of fish at her feet.

The river woman plucked another trout from her hair and raised her arm. "Find another place to camp, you overrated princess!"

This fish sailed over Emily's head towards the woman on land, who whacked it with her paddle and sent it back. "That's *Queen Ella* to you," she snarled.

Emily bent to scoop up the fish that had smacked her in the face and returned it to the water, then crab-walked out of the line of fire. The meadow was in late-season bloom, insects buzzing between sweet-smelling flowers. It was exactly as depicted in the painting, if she ignored the screaming women and flying fish; a new one, even for her.

A pair of raccoons lingered nearby in a patch of red clover, attention focused on the turmoil. She wasn't particularly skilled at communicating cross-species, but as luck would have it, part of her toolkit included a translation runestone fashioned by a fellow witch with a gift for language. She pulled it out of her bag and turned to address the raccoons.

"Hello, friends! My name is Emily Fairweather. I've been sent by the Order of Panacea to help with, um..." She waved her hand in the general direction of the mayhem. "...that." The fish catcher was now plucking trout from her bucket and using the paddle to bat them in quick succession at the woman in the water, who was alternating between throwing and ducking. "Any chance you can fill me in on the problem?"

The two raccoons looked at each other, then at Emily. In unison, they extended little paws in the direction of her bag.

"Right. Snacks." Emily dug around to find half a peanut butter sandwich, a stale tea biscuit, and a piece of chick'n jerky. One of the raccoons snatched the sandwich, the other grabbed the tea biscuit. The jerky received a sniff of disdain, apparently not good enough for the selective palates of food scavengers. Fair enough—it wasn't Emily's favourite either.

After a brief moment of munching, the raccoons—Bob and Greta—began to chitter, snort, whimper, and snarl, filling Emily in on the history of the past several days.

The woman standing in the water had arrived first. She was there for five days, no six, no it was definitely five days —Bob and Greta seemed to have their own struggles with bickering—and spent most of her time up in the branches of a tall oak tree near the water, singing songs and brushing her long hair. Such long hair, tangled in everything. Greta felt it was ridiculous when a person with so much hair also had a problem with excessive shedding. Perhaps this woman needed a good grooming session. Bob said not everyone cared about grooming as much as Greta did, and gave a look that suggested this was not the first time the two had discussed this particular issue. Greta ignored him, continuing her report.

The second woman arrived and set up camp in the field a few days after the first. The new arrival spent her days in a canoe on the river, which she put into the water each morning and carried back at the end of each day. Bob, chittering with open-mouthed glee, called it her boat-hat. Wasn't it funny to wear a boat as a hat? Not something you'd see on a raccoon, Greta agreed. The pair declared it ironic that humans called raccoons trashy while they walked around wearing boats and shedding hair. Emily agreed—humans *were* an endless source of amusement.

Bob and Greta said that all was well until it wasn't. The women went from friends to foes, becoming very disruptive. Couldn't they at least keep the volume down in the morning? The free fish were appreciated, though.

With that, Greta collected a fish that flopped a little too long in the grass and scurried off to the tree line to find some peace. Bob followed in quick pursuit.

Emily was not quite sure what to make of this information, but she did know what to do next: brew a pot of tea.

The campsite was located a few yards from the battlefield. The area had two large canvas tents and a small twig-constructed shelf, which contained a pot, two plates, four cups, and three baskets. There was, as Greta suggested, a great deal of loose hair lying about. Strands were tangled on tent poles and coiled in the fire pit. A few strays even attempted to work their way inside Emily's shoes.

A yelp sounded across the field, pulling Emily's attention from the camp inventory. The women were engaged in a tug of war over a long lock of hair that stretched out of the water and up to the bucket of fish on the bank of the river. It appeared to have a life of its own as it wiggled about, attempting to wrap itself around the neck of the assailant that dared to pull its end. Emily assessed that they wouldn't manage to kill each other in the next few minutes and got to work setting a fire.

She used some kindling and a touch of magic to start a flame, and pulled a collection of dried herbs from her bag: chamomile to soothe frayed nerves, mint to cool heated tempers, hibiscus to sweeten the mood. When the pot of tea was at a simmer, she turned to wave her arms at the still-fighting women.

"Yoo hoo! Friends! Hello!" Emily's chipper voice rang out across the field. The two women—now half-heartedly waving the fish at each other—turned in her direction.

"Join me for a cup of tea, won't you?"

The promise of a refreshing beverage was enough to pull them away from their battle. Emily directed them to log seats around the fire, ensuring the two women would be as far from each other as possible. She handed each a cup of fragrant tea and waited for them to take their first sip.

"Let's start with introductions, shall we? I'm Emily." She took a swallow of her own tea. "I was sent by the Order of Panacea."

The canoer jolted upright on her seat. "The Order of *Panacea*? The *witch's* order? Why would they send you here?" Her voice, without the edge of bickering, was melodious. "Not that you're unwelcome, of course." Someone must have taught her that manners were always important when dealing with witches.

"Well, it appears some *order* is needed here, wouldn't you say?" Emily cocked an eyebrow and shifted her gaze between the two women perched on their logs. "Alas, I am never told the specifics of why, my dear. I just go where I am directed. And who are we to question the motives of the Order?"

"Right, of course. I didn't mean—" The woman's voice quavered and a bead of sweat appeared on her brow. "Excuse me. Ella. My name. I'm Ella."

Emily reached out to clasp Ella's hand and was met with a strong grip and calloused fingers. "Don't be alarmed by the stories you've heard," she said. "The tales about the Order are often exaggerated to encourage the cooperation of unruly children. We're really not so bad." Emily winked and gave Ella's hand a final pat. "Most of us, anyway."

"Yes, of course." Ella's shoulders dropped a fraction.

"I'm Rapunzel." The other woman interjected, offering Emily a rather hairy hand, which came as no surprise at all.

"Pleased to meet you both," Emily said. "Now, from what I've witnessed so far, it appears I'm here to help resolve a conflict."

"A resolution is easy," said Rapunzel. "Tell that trespasser to get out of my campsite. Problem solved." She flicked a section of hair from her shoulder. The wet tendril sent river-water flying towards Ella, who issued a low growl in response.

"*Me* leave? I booked this spot months ago, which you well know. Your time was up days back. It's *you* who needs to leave." Ella kicked a pebble into Rapunzel's hair, which stretched to encircle the firepit.

"I was here first. I'm not going anywhere. Squatter's rights." Rapunzel flicked another strand of hair at Ella. The two women moved to stand.

"Enough of that, please." Emily tapped into the absolute authority of stern mothers and headmistresses everywhere, making the demand impossible to ignore. Lacing her voice with a little magic helped, of course.

They immediately settled back onto their seats, heads bowed, hands cradling cups of tea in their laps.

"I understand you were both getting along just fine for a while, yes? Best of friends and all that?"

Both women made sounds of agreement.

"So," Emily asked, "what do you think changed?"

"Well, you try living with her. There's hair everywhere and —"

"She sings all the time, calling the birds who crap every —."

"At least I have *friends*!"

"At least my husband doesn't have a *foot fetish*!"

Emily raised a hand for silence. "Right. Well. Something has gone wrong here, causing..." She motioned between them. "...all of this."

She reached into her bag for a clear quartz runestone. "Let's test for a curse, shall we?"

Starting at Ella's feet and working up to the top of her head, Emily scanned the stone over the woman's body. It flickered with blue swirls as it read her aura, but there was no buzzing or heat or putrid yellow that would indicate a curse. Emily repeated the process with Rapunzel, receiving only lilac sparks.

"Not a curse," she proclaimed, dropping the stone back into her bag. She was relieved, as breaking curses often took a great deal of time, and she was already pining for her favourite chair.

"Have either of you entered into a contract with an especially beautiful or particularly terrifying creature?"

Both women shook their heads, no.

"No back-alley deals? Wishes for your heart's desire that caused a magical helper to appear, creating mayhem?"

Ella cleared her throat. "Well, I did make a wish once to go to a ball, and my fairy godmother caused a bit of a stir with the glass slippers she gave me. But that was ages ago. She's always been lovely. And a little odd. More lovely than odd." Ella took a gulp of her tea. Her face took on a sour expression that Emily knew was not caused by the brew. "That's how I met my husband."

"Ah, yes. Fairy godmothers are harmless. Or at least, harmless to their charges. Or not harmful-on-purpose, anyway. And you say it was ages ago, so I doubt that's the problem." Emily reached out to pat Ella's hand, which was clutching the cup in a vise-like grip. "Or not *this* problem, in any case."

"Husbands." Rapunzel said. "That's the problem, for sure."

Emily turned to her. "Hmm. Do you feel your husband may have done something to cause this strife? Any chance he slipped discontentment powders into your travel food?"

"Food? He wouldn't know the first thing about preparing food," Rapunzel muttered. "Maybe if he had a hobby like cooking—or anything at all, really—he wouldn't be such a bore, and I wouldn't need to go camping to escape him." A flush of red bloomed high in her cheeks. "Not that it's any relief to be suffering through days listening to this one," she raised her chin in the direction of Ella, "talking non-stop about her perfect life with her perfect gardens and perfect rat hotel."

"They are not rats, they are mice! And they deserve beautiful accommodations for staying by my side through everything. For remaining true friends—unlike you!"

"Ha! How would you know what true friendship looks like?" Rapunzel placed her cup on the ground and rose to her feet. "You ate all the chocolate; didn't leave me any! You knew how much I was looking forward to it," she growled.

"It was *my* chocolate! And you ate all the berries *and* the cheese!" Ella jumped to her feet, still gripping her now-empty cup.

"Maybe you can get some more cheese from your *rats*."

Emily pulled out her flask of elderberry wine and took a swig, grateful to her past self for the foresight. A warm flush washed over her as she listened to the women bicker over whether or not mice made better companions than people and deserved to sleep in tiny mice beds. Moments like this made her appreciate that she lived alone. Though she did wonder if she should create a nicer space for the critters that sometimes popped in for a visit.

She felt a tug at her skirt. Bob and Greta were back from their excursion in the woods, once again enjoying the show. Bob scurried over to the cooking shelf and knocked the lid off a basket beside the plates. It was filled with dried orange mushrooms.

"Clever Bob!" Emily patted him on the head. "Did you know these were here the whole time?"

Bob moved his hand in what Emily took to be the equivalent of a shrug and turned his back. She didn't bother to ask why he hadn't pointed out the mushrooms during their first conversation. Raccoons had a bit of the trickster in them, and who was she to judge him for his entertainment?

She held the basket out to the women. "Have you been eating these?"

"Yes, we foraged them in the woods," Ella said.

"They're chanterelles," Rapunzel added.

"Oh no. Not chanterelles." Emily picked up a shriveled specimen and sniffed. "I think we've solved our mystery, friends. These are jack o' lanterns." She ran a hand over the mushroom. It plumped up, gills expanded as if it were just picked from the ground. "You're lucky the impact was a mere ornery mood, as the physical effects for non-magical folks can be quite unpleasant."

"Non-magical folks?" Rapunzel asked.

"Yes. The folks who don't have magic. Unlike all of us."

"All of us?" Ella looked around as if expecting someone new to jump from behind the tent.

"Yes, us." Emily swept her hand about to indicate all three of them.

The two women stared at her, eyes vacant of comprehension.

"Friends, the Order doesn't send me out for non-magical support. Imagine the workload, what with all the nonsense humans get up to." Emily laughed. "You're witches. Obviously."

The women turned to Emily in unison. "*Witches*?"

"Come now. Did you think it was normal to communicate with animals or have hair that fetches things for you?" Emily clucked her tongue. "I dare say you're both smarter than that."

"What does—"

"How do we—"

"Will the Order—"

Emily waved her hands for silence. "Now, now. Let's get this mushroom fog all sorted. There will be plenty of time for questions when you have your heads on straight."

It took two days of bitter potions, herbal soaks, and sunbathing in the middle of elaborate crystal grids to get the women back to their normal, chipper selves. When all was settled, Emily kept her promise, answering the women's questions as best she could, which was admittedly not very well at all.

"What does the Order actually do?" asked Rapunzel.

"It keeps everyone in order."

"But, *how* does it do that?" asked Ella.

"Oh, a little of this, a little of that. Some of us keep an eye on things to spot any problems. Some of us are sent out to fix those problems. Others play different roles."

"What types of roles?"

"I can't really say. And even if I could, I wouldn't. It's a process of discovery that every witch must experience on their own. Your role might be no role at all, other than the one you are living right now."

"When will we know if we're to have a role?"

"That depends."

"How will we know?"

"That also depends."

"What does it depend on?"

"The type of role you're given."

This circular conversation went on for a while. It was a testament to the natural temperament of all involved that no one stomped off in a huff or resumed throwing fish. Eventually, the women decided they had enough non-answers and accepted that they'd be told what they needed to know when they needed to know it.

With that, it was time to head home. Emily could feel her rose garden calling, and she had certainly earned some time with her book.

"Thank you, Emily. We will be forever grateful," said Ella.

"Please do say we'll see you again," said Rapunzel.

Emily clasped a hand from each. "You have only to wish for me and set out on a path. When you stumble upon my tea shop, I will have a cup ready for you."

She bent down to address Bob and Greta, who had scurried over to say goodbye. "You too, little friends."

Emily pulled the painting of her small tea shop out of her bag, sprinkled some gold travel dust, and focused on home. As she drifted away, she thought perhaps the best part of being in company was that it helped you appreciate solitude all the more.

Melanie Mulrooney lives in Nova Scotia with her husband and a gaggle of kids. Her work has been published with Elegant Literature, EGG+FROG, TL;DR Press, and others. When not writing or child-wrangling, she can be found reading, volunteering in her community, or strolling through the woods—usually with a cup of tea in hand, and always wearing comfortable shoes. She finds writing bios much harder than writing stories.

Find her at melmulrooney.com or on Bluesky @melmulrooney.bsky.social

Wizarding
by Nicole Walsh

Zilchramy Blackhammer scuffed his way out of his neat, orderly bedroom. Morning. Too sunny. Too bright. And the birds! What was Adaline thinking, setting bird-feeders outside every window?

Mornings, the elderly necromancer decided, were going to become Points Of Discussion. He had his notebook and pen tucked into the deep pocket of his second-most-glittery house-robe. Adaline and Zilchramy had agreed to meet once a week to table emerging issues.

Sunlight blasted through every uncurtained window in the echoey, wooden house. Quite a feat, considering the gutter-rotting trees poking in every which way. The hallway carpet was faded, worn, and edged with dust. What did the woman have against housework?

"Compromise," Zilchramy frowned. "Evolving."

As he scuffed his way down the hall to the bathroom they would *not* be sharing, his foot skitched a rumple in the rug. He staggered forward, nearly flying straight through the filthy glass of the window.

"Adaline!" he roared. "A bit of common sense!"

"What?" Adaline Dawnsparrow's unmusical voice rose from the adjacent bedroom, where she started clattering and battering about predawn.

"Trip hazard!" he shouted.

"Those slippers? I told you not to wear those slippers!"

"I am not wearing the slippers!" Zilchramy stumbled on the bathroom mat, inexplicably bundled on the floor. It tripped him into the shower stall, tangling him in the non-too-clean curtain.

"The mess on you!" he shouted.

"I'm not up yet."

"What?"

"I am not *up* yet," Adaline roared. "Which means it's *your* mess, in *your* bathroom, you incongruous old *fool!*"

"My bathroom?" Zilchramy thundered. "I moved in last night. This mat was most certainly not...! Ack!" The shower curtain sucked in against his face.

"I cannot hear you!" Adaline shouted.

"Mmmmrfthh!"

"I cannot hear you."

The elderly necromancer peeled the plastic off his face to screech: "Trying to kill me!"

"Such nonsense!" Adaline's voice sounded distant, from the kitchen. "No animal products, I said. Don't be stomping your dead nasty skins about the floor and you'll be fine!"

Zilchramy ack-ed, floundering. His grotty, steel-rimmed fingernails skittered across tiles.

"Stop banging about!" Adaline shouted. "It's an old house. You'll break something." An unquiet grumble, "Quiet and keeps to himself, indeed."

Zilchramy tore free of the curtain, diving toward the bathroom door. A new rumple in the carpet tripped him out the door and into the glass of the window, which unlatched and popped open, nearly tumbling him headfirst into the garden.

"The drama on you," Adaline shouted. "It's not going to work, Zilchramy. Not if you're going to behave like this every morning."

"A curse!" Zilchramy shouted. "A spell. Adaline!"

"No spells!" she shouted. "The house doesn't like wizards!"

"I'm not..." Zilchramy heaved his top half back in the window, dazed, blinded by sunlight. He paused. Checking his body. He was, in fact, wearing his bone-beaded, glitter-studded house-robe.

He edged the bathroom a look.

"Alright," he said. "Look. Taking it off. See?"

He shrugged the robe off. Displayed it to the open window. The hall. Moving cautiously, he inched into the bathroom in his boxer shorts and singlet.

"Not wizarding," Zilchramy soothed. "Not in the house. See?"

He hung his robe up.

It dropped from the hook. Onto the floor. Into a puddle.

"Really mature," Zilchramy huffed.

He eased to the toilet, moving slowly. Nothing untoward happening. He did what was required.

"Damnable house," he growled. The moment he touched the tap, water exploded, splashed about the basin, soaking his crotch.

He shrieked.

"Zilchramy!" Adaline shouted. "The noises you make!"

The elderly necromancer studied his soaked pants. The curtain rustled. Zilchramy bolted.

"Stupid damn... aaaargh!" he tripped and flailed into the kitchen, snicking scratches down the wallpaper of the hall with his clawlike nails. "Damnation!"

"Not in the house, please!" Adaline stood at the sink, wreathed in sunlight. Dazed bees circled her head. Birds eyed them from the window ledge, pooping into the sink.

"The house is trying to kill me!"

"Coming into a room like that, no wonder." The herb-witch flinched. "The face on you! Not a morning person, are you?"

"Necromancer," he growled.

"Not in the house... GODDESS, are you naked?"

"I'm not wizarding, Adaline!" Zilchramy's toe slammed into a stool: "OUCH!"

"A bit less screaming, please."

"Something's wrong with your house!" he gasped.

"Well. The new lodger seems somewhat subpar," she said.

Zilchramy wrenched open the fridge. He took out the orange juice, shaking it vigorously. The lid sailed off. Orange juice sprayed the length of the kitchen. Zilchramy stared.

Adaline took a sip of tea, saying *nothing* (in a very loud way).

"That lid was on!" he squeaked.

Adaline's lips compressed.

"Zil," Adaline said, very carefully.

"Addy," he snarled. "No. I'm not wearing the robes. Or the shoes. Or, 'wizarding about the place'. Whatever that entails."

Adaline set her cup down. She gave him a look. "One has to ask, Zilchramy..."

"I prefer you did not," he growled.

"Did you *perhaps*, get out of the wrong side of the bed today?"

Zilchramy glowered.

"I was tired," he said. "My back hurts. It's discombobulating, moving house at this age. Moving in with a woman you like after decades of being single. Realising your partner may have certain habits..."

"Like wandering about in his boxers?" Adaline proposed.

"Like not vacuuming the edges. Not putting lids on bottles. So yes, Adaline, maybe I was in a bit of a glowery mood."

"Hmm," Adaline said.

"Hmmm?"

"Hmm," she agreed. "Also. Perhaps. Did you get out of the wrong side of the actual bed? I told you to sleep on the window side? Pause to greet the day?"

"It's my bed," Zilchramy grumped. "I will decide what side of the..." He paused, considering. "Is... that a thing?"

Adaline edged a shrug.

"Ah." Zilchramy deflated. "Would it help, perhaps, if I went back and exited differently?"

"I don't imagine it would hurt."

Zilchramy eyed the stove, the kettle, the knives. "In the meantime, perhaps..."

"I will make the breakfast," she agreed. "We could take it in turns."

"Or, I the lunch, and you, the breakfasts?"

"That sounds reasonable."

Nicole Walsh (she/her) is a cat enthusiast from the east coast of Australia who loves fern gardens and long dresses. She writes short and novel-length speculative fiction and urban fantasy that span from a little bit dark, a little bit amusing through to a little bit steamy. Her work features in 50+ magazines and anthologies. Her second novel, sci-fi-fantasy mashup novel The God-Wife Reborn is OUT NOW.

Visit Nicole at: https://nicolewalshauthor.com/

Testify
by Thomas J. Misuraca

"Friends!" Maribel summoned the courage to step into the aisle of the tiny church that was filled to the brim with worshipers. "I would like to share my story."

"Preach it, sister!" somebody behind her responded.

"We're listening!" somebody in front of her encouraged.

She took a deep, diaphragmatic breath, then began to speak: "Just one year ago I was not the same person you see standing in front of you. I was what some would call a big-old-mess. I was down on my luck and at the end of my rope."

"Been there!"

"I started out as a good little girl. A straight A student, who tutored other students and was involved in tons of school activities. The preteen every neighbor trusted to babysit their kids. And of course I went to church with my parents ever Sunday."

"Amen!"

"But deep inside me, I felt an itch. A dark desire for something more. Little did I realize I was being led into temptation by…" She paused. "Satan."

At the mention of that name, the room erupted with screams, moans and boos.

"I know, I know, it's a tale as old as time. The good teenage girl suddenly wanting to rebel against her parents."

"Honor thy mother and father!"

"I should have. But instead I did everything they taught me not to do. I got in with a bad crowd. I'd skip my tutoring sessions to drink with them in the woods. I'd blow off babysitting and go to wild parties on the bad side of town. There, I'd take any drug that was offered to me."

"Satan's poison!"

"I couldn't get high enough. Trying to sooth that Satanic itch. I'd take drugs morning, noon and night. At first, men gave them to me for free in exchange for sexual favors."

"Devils!"

"But when that tap ran dry, I did whatever I could to get money for drugs. I'd steal from my parents, friends and family. I'd beg on the street corners. And at my lowest, I'd prostitute myself."

"For shame!"

"My family threw me out of the house and my friends abandoned me. I was expelled from school, not that I was going anymore anyhow. I ended up living on the street. Life literally kicked me into the gutter."

"Poor lost soul!"

"But one day, when I was at my lowest, I heard a voice calling to me. It was a cross between a whisper and a boisterous baritone. It felt so warm and loving, it thawed my ice-cold body. It said I was his child and he was here to guide me back to the light. That voice was… Jesus!"

The crown went wild.

"Amen!"

"Praise him!"

"From the middle of the darkness around me, I saw a hand reach out. It was bathed in a bright white light. As I reached for it, I felt myself lifting out of the gutter. Almost floating on air. The light encompassed me. And, like an arm around my shoulders, it led me to the local church church where good people took me in. They fed me, clothed me and made me feel like part of the community."

"Amen!"

"Jesus' voice continued to guide me into making better choices. He'd work in mysterious ways, having pamphlets for continuing education show up in the mail. Then helped me receive scholarships. Guidance councilors guided by his hand suggested I go into teaching. And now I'm helping to guide the next generation into his arms."

"Hallelujah!"

"He keeps me nourished with his love. And has brought me more joy than any drug I'd ever taken."

"He's nourished you!"

"I'm thankful every day for my second chance."

"Amen!"

"I know many of you had similar low points, and learned Jesus never abandons us. He carries us to where we need to be. Today, I am here with my new family and reunited with my old. Knowing if I ever stray again, all I have to do is listen for his voice and let his warm hands guide me. Thank you Jesus! Amen!"

Responses echoed through the church. Strangers reached out to touch and hug her.

"Thank you for sharing your story."

"We're so happy you are here with us."

"You're an inspiration."

And as the next person began to tell their story, she quietly slipped out of the church.

She walked briskly down the street. After a moment, she took out her phone and called Susan, who was anxious to hear the results.

"It went great! They bought that monologue. Every word. So yeah, her character is quite believable. We'll find another church to test out that character dealing with a teen pregnancy. This is going to be a great show! See you at rehearsal."

Thomas J. Misuraca studied Writing, Publishing and Literature at Emerson College in his home town of Boston. After graduation, he moved to Los Angeles where he splits his time between writing and graphic design. Over 160 of his short stories and two novels have been published. He was nominated for a Pushcart Prize in 2021. He is also a multi-award winning playwright with over 170 short plays and 14 full-lengths produced globally. His musical, Geeks!, was produced Off-Broadway in May 2019.

The Spinning Wheel
by Maureen Bowden

'Merrily, cheeringly, noiselessly whirring
Spins the wheel, rings the wheel while the foot's stirring'
(The Spinning Wheel: John Francis Waller)

Saturday morning, Eileen's eyes were drawn to the ancient, spinning wheel in the window of 'James Malone Antiques', known to the local populace as 'Jimmy's Junk'. The dusty artefact reminded her of a song her mother would sing to her when she was a child. The girl in the song, also called Eileen, sat spinning under the sharp ears of her blind grandmother. When the old lady fell asleep, the naughty minx scuttled off for a bit of slap and tickle with her boyfriend, a minstrel boy. The story had always made Eileen giggle and the thought of the minstrel boy had given her a strange tingle she rather liked.

She felt an odd compulsion to buy the spinning wheel. After the usual haggling with wiry-haired, worldly-wise Jimmy Malone, he sold it to her for half the asking price and a discount on the delivery charge. They shook hands and she left the shop, somewhat bewildered. Why had she done that? It would certainly be what interior decorators refer to as a conversation piece, but there had to be more to her compulsion.

On Saturday afternoon, two of Jimmy's heavies arrived in his delivery rust bucket and hauled the spinning wheel up two flights of stairs to the student flat she shared with her friend, Sophie. Following Eileen's instructions they dumped it in the space between the traffic cone and Piers Bones, a plastic skeleton wearing a beret.

Sophie surveyed the new conversation piece. "Cool, but you can clean it. I'm not going anywhere near it with a feather duster." She sashayed out, bedecked in Lycra, bling and false lashes resembling tarantulas sitting on her eyelids. "I'm off to an all-night party so don't wait up."

Eileen called, "Have fun but don't get any more tattoos like last time and try not to catch anything."

Turning her attention back to the spinning wheel, she gasped. A strange woman was sitting at it. Regal and ageless, she smiled but was terrifying. Eileen wanted to run off to the party with Sophie but she was unable to move. Trembling, she said, "Who are you? Why are you here?"

The woman laughed. "Calm down, girl. You're safer with me than with that flibbertigibbet. I am *The Spinner of the Fabric of Time*. In Gaelic myth I am called **Moirai**."

Eileen shook her head. "Never heard of you."

"Ah, well, I have many names. To name a few, I was Clotho, one of the Three Fates, to the ancient Greeks; Nona to the Romans; and Verdandi to the Nordic folk."

"Okay, but you haven't told me why you're here. What do you want with me?"

"You have torn a hole in the Fabric of Time and you must repair it. Of course, you'll have to leave this place for a while but you shouldn't miss all this junk." She stared at Piers. "And that gentleman deserves a decent burial."

Eileen was close to panic. "I'm not going anywhere. I haven't torn the fabric of anything, my conversation pieces aren't junk and the skeleton isn't even real—it's plastic."

"Everything is real, Eileen A' Roon."

"Why do you call me that?"

"Because that is who you are: the girl in the spinning wheel song. It's what Caral O'Daly, her minstrel boy, called her. It means 'Eileen, My Love'. I'll send you back to your previous life in the seventeenth century so you can see the damage you did. Of course, it was partly your father's fault.

If the stupid man hadn't made such an unnecessary fuss about whom you could or couldn't marry the problem would never have occurred. Anyway, it's up to you to fix it. While you're there you'll remember your life here as only a dream."

She was beginning to wonder if *this* was the dream. "How will you do that? Do you have a time machine?"

"I need only my spinning wheel. When I turn it in reverse time unravels, but don't worry, when I turn it forward again it will bring you back."

A swirling light engulfed Eileen. She closed her eyes against it and fell backwards onto her dilapidated but cosy couch.

When she opened her eyes, she was riding on horseback alongside her parents, Master and Mistress Cavannah of Clonnmullen Castle, County Carlow, south east of Ireland. They were on their way to Carrickduff Castle, the abode of Master and Mistress McCann, to attend the wedding of the McCann's son, Roddy.

Eileen's father called to her. "I had Roddy McCann in mind for you, but I left my negotiations too late. I won't make that mistake again. There are plenty of young noblemen in need of a bride. I have a few candidates to consider."

Eileen silently screamed. Why should it bother him who she married? It was her life. Forcing herself to be calm, she whispered to her mother, "I'd prefer to choose my own husband, Mama."

Her mother shook her head, "You're not a peasant to be rolled in the hay by a farmhand, Eileen. You're nobility. Your marriage must be appropriately arranged."

Eileen said nothing. This was ridiculous. It wouldn't happen. She'd make sure of that.

After Roddy's wedding ceremony the guests gathered for the celebrations in the castle's Great Hall. Master McCann addressed them, "We will now be entertained by the greatest harper in the land. May I introduce Caral O'Daly?"

Eileen gasped. She knew that name, but from where? Was it a true memory or a dream? She let the music of his harp possess her: the light and shade of lilting melody fulfilling her need for joy and hope. She couldn't take her eyes from the young man and she was aware he was watching her.

During the mid-evening break in the entertainment he passed close to her as he was leaving the hall and whispered, "The garden."

Her parents were in conversation with a rich, local chieftain, no doubt arranging her marriage to one of his offspring. They didn't see her slip away. Caral was waiting for her. He took her in his arms and kissed her.

In the following weeks they met secretly at every opportunity, but scandal spreads like manure that feeds the crops. A furious Master Cavannah confronted her. "You have brought shame onto the Cavannah clan. You will be confined within these castle walls until I have finalised your marriage negotiations."

Taking her out of anyone's hearing, her mother whispered, "Did you permit him to take your maidenhead?"

Eileen crossed her fingers behind her back and replied, "No, Mother."

One sleepless night as she lay weeping, she heard a knock on her bedroom door and Maeve, the scullery-maid came in. "Mistress," she said, "you must dress and come to the kitchens. The minstrel boy is here. I won't tell anyone."

With her heart pounding, Eileen dressed and crept to the kitchen. Caral, with his harp at his side as always, was sitting at the ancient oak table. He ran to her and before she could speak he said, "Before I explain how I managed to be here I must ask you, Eileen A'Roon, will you marry me?"

She laughed, "Of course I will, but how can I escape my father?"

"Come and sit down, I'll explain."

She sat.

"My patron, Master McCann, will help us. There is an underground tunnel between this castle and his. I came through it. These tunnels aren't unusual. They're escape routes from castles under siege in wartime. The entrances are in the dungeons."

She nodded. "I've heard my mother speak of it, but I didn't know where it led."

"We must leave tonight. Master McCann has sent for a priest. He will arrive tomorrow and he will marry us."

He stood and picked up the lantern resting on the table. "It's dark in the tunnel. I brought this."

She took the lantern, he took his harp, and they descended the dank, stone stairway into the dungeon. They reached the tunnel entrance, but before they stepped in she called, "Wait, Caral. What's that?" She held the lantern high. Further along the dungeon wall was the entrance to another tunnel. "When my father finds I'm missing he's bound to know where I've gone. He'll follow us and try to take me back, but who knows where that other tunnel will lead? If it takes us somewhere far away we'll be free of him. Please, let's try it. We can always come back and take the one to Carrickduff Castle if we don't like what we find."

Before waiting for his reply she ran into the other tunnel and he followed her. They were swept along in a rolling rainbow, buffeted by a warm wind until they emerged from an ancient tumulus and stepped out onto rough grassland beyond a rocky shoreline. A band of warriors armed with spears, swords, and javelins approached. The leader greeted them, "I am Carthy, chieftain of my clan. Who are you?"

Caral replied. "I am a minstrel, Caral of the O'Daly clan. This is Eileen, my betrothed. I see you are prepared for battle. Who are your enemies?"

"The Dumnoni tribe from the southwest of Albion. The hordes of Rome are trampling and slashing their way across their land so they're escaping from them and coming here by sea to trample and slash their own way across our land of Erin. Our lookout is in place to warn us of their next landing."

Caral whispered to her, "That tunnel's led us back through time to the first century after the life of Christ."

She whispered back, "Well, my father won't find us here. He won't know where to start looking." She turned to Carthy. "The Dumnoni need your help. Why won't you offer them friendship and shelter?"

"They're savages, Lady. What do you know of such things? We have to kill them before they kill us"

"They probably think the same about you. If you would talk to them you might not need to kill each other."

"Does that plan work where you come from?"

She turned to Caral. He shook his head. They said in unison, "Not always."

The chieftain laughed. "It seldom does. When the Dumnoni arrive, run for your lives, unless the music of a harp can charm away their savagery."

Caral said. "He's right, Eileen. We must get as far away from the coast as possible."

They had no time to run. The look-out called, "They come. They're led by archers." Arrows flew and battle raged. Caral died in Eileen's arms with a Dumnoni arrow through his heart. She closed her eyes and howled.

Moirai's voice rang in her head. "Shut up, girl. Leave the keening to the Banshee. I'll take you home."

Eileen heard the whirring of the wheel rolling forwards and when she opened her eyes, she was back in her flat. Trembling, she said. "It was my fault. I led Caral to his death. I shouldn't have taken that strange tunnel."

Moirai said. "Of course you shouldn't. The tumulus into which it led was a centre of ancient magic. Those places must be treated with caution and respect. You were meant to take the man-made tunnel to Carrickduff Castle, marry Caral O'Daly and have four children with him. You deprived them and all their descendants of the lives they should have lived."

"So that's the hole I tore in the fabric of time?"

"It is and you must repair it."

"Are you going to send me back to the tunnel?"

"I am. I'm giving you a chance to put this right. Take it, Eileen A' Roon."

Once again, the wheel whirred in reverse and time unravelled. She was standing with Caral at the entrance to the tunnel that led to Carrickduff Castle. She saw the other tunnel and a chill of fear sent a shiver along her spine. The words, 'caution and respect', echoed in her head. Why? Was this another intrusion of a dream, as when she first saw Caral? Whatever it was she needed to get away from it. Holding the lantern high she made her way with her minstrel to Carrickduff Castle.

Mistress McCann ushered them into separate bedrooms. "You'll not share a bed under my roof until you've made your vows before a priest. He'll be here after breakfast."

Father Malone was a wiry little man with worldly wisdom in his piercing eyes. Once again a feeling of familiarity nudged Eileen's consciousness—she was learning to ignore it. He led the way to the castle's chapel and after all appropriate words had been said he pronounced them husband and wife.

Master Cavannah burst into the chapel. "Step away from that minstrel, Eileen. Whatever vows you've made, your union has not been consummated and it never will be!"

Master McCann placed himself between Eileen and her irate father. "Don't be a fool, Master Cavannah. You should be grateful your child will spend her life with a minstrel. My son, Roddy, although only recently married, is fighting the English invaders. He risks losing his life and leaving his young bride in widowhood. I wish he'd chosen a harp, instead of a sword."

Master Cavannah shook his head. "Your son can do as he pleases, Master McCann, but my daughter will do as I say."

Father Malone pointed an accusing finger at him. "What the almighty has joined together, let no man put asunder."

Master Cavannah roared, "Look around you, Father. There are sunderings everywhere."

The priest appeared to grow to twice his size and his voice boomed and echoed from wall to wall. "Well, there'll be none here. This man and woman are soul mates. They were meant to be together so hold your blethering tongue. My roar is louder than yours."

Master Cavannah, his arrogance quelled, cowered and fell silent.

Father Malone was unlike any priest Eileen had ever encountered. Was he something older and more mysterious? She didn't care. Whatever he was, he'd defeated her father.

Eileen and Caral had a long, happy life. Their four children thrived and had families of their own. When Eileen, in old age, drew her final breath and closed her eyes, she heard Moirai's voice. "You have done well. Now it's time for you to leave."

Sunday morning, she opened her eyes. Sitting on the couch in her student flat, she experienced the contentment of awakening from a long, happy dream. The grotesque, multicoloured cuckoo clock—another purchase from 'Jimmy's Junk'—perched on the windowsill, showed the time, ten-thirty. Eileen's journey into the past had lasted all night and half the morning.

Moirai was smiling.

Eileen smiled back. "Did I fix it?"

"You did. Descendents of Eileen and Caral are alive today. You are one of those descendants but you are also a reincarnation of Eileen A'Roon. Mortals live many lives in order to learn many lessons."

"If I've reincarnated, has Caral?"

"He has."

"Will I meet him again?"

"Of course you will. Soul mates always find each other. Now I must leave you. Goodbye Eileen." She vanished. So did the spinning wheel.

Sunday afternoon, Sophie returned. Somewhat dishevelled and with one tarantula missing, she shimmered through the space between the traffic cone and Piers Bones before flopping onto the couch.

Eileen said. "I sent it back."

Sophie frowned. "You sent what back?"

"The spinning wheel, of course."

"Spinning wheel? What ya talking about? Someone must have spiked your cornflakes. Anyway, never mind that. I met a really cool guy at the party and invited him round here tonight. He's bringing a friend for you."

"Oh, no he's not. I don't want a blind date with any specimen of your acquaintance."

"You'll like this one. He's really cute, his name's Carl and he plays the guitar real good."

A sudden movement caught Eileen's eye. She glanced at Piers. One of his lidless eye sockets appeared to flicker. She could have sworn he winked.

Maureen Bowden is a Liverpudlian, living with her musician husband in North Wales. She has had 227 stories and poems accepted by paying markets including Third Flatiron, Water Dragon Publishing, The First Line and many others. She was nominated for the 2015 international Pushcart Prize and in 2019 Hiraeth Books published an anthology of her stories, 'Whispers of Magic.' They plan to publish an anthology of her poetry in the near future. She also writes song lyrics, mostly comic political satire, set to traditional melodies and her husband has performed them in folk music clubs throughout the UK. She loves her family and friends, rock 'n' roll, Shakespeare, and cats.

Full Stop
by Gregg Chamberlain

Well, here I am at last, where no one has been before, at the very end of the Universe. And what do I find? A large sign with big red letters that reads "Stop Infinity".

Okay, so now where do I go from here then?

Gregg Chamberlain writes speculative fiction for fun, and zombie filk because he can. He lives in rural Eastern Ontario, Canada, with his missus, Anne, and their cats, who allow the humans the run of the house.

is...

/ˈfo͞ofəˌrô/
noun:

1. *a great deal of fuss or attention given to a minor matter;*
2. *showy frills added unnecessarily;*
3. *a zine and indie publisher of surreal storytelling and worldly observations.*

Masthead

Kevin Kortum, *Chief exaggeration officer*

Tony Tran, *Director of superfluous beauty*

Jeff Goldberg, *Editor-at-ease*

H. Marin, *Master of minutiae*

Megan Diedericks, *Social chronicler of minor disturbances*

and as always
be kind, stay sane